She'd never been kissed.

Until now.

Anything she might have imagined as a young girl didn't even begin to scratch the surface. She felt disoriented and yet there was this wild rush inside her. And electricity. A great deal of electricity, crackling and humming between them. It took everything Claire had not to just fall into the kiss and remain there.

But she couldn't. It wasn't right. This wasn't what she'd intended to happen.

Her breath felt trapped in her throat. And she was dizzy. She, who had never been lost for words, now felt as if she'd suddenly been struck dumb.

Dear Reader,

For those Catholic children whose parents couldn't afford a parochial education, there was "religious instructions" or, as some of us called it, "catechism." We studied our book, memorizing answers to questions just in case, when we finally made it up to the Pearly Gates, St. Peter decided to give us a quiz. We all went on Saturdays and Wednesdays. It was Wednesdays that made us a source of envy for the other students. They had to remain seated while we—they thought—ran off to freedom when the bell rang dismissing "all students attending religious instructions." The truth was, we remained captives of these sharp-witted, often sharp-tongued ladies whose faces and hands were the only visible evidence that they were human rather than spirits sent by God to tidy up our immortal souls.

I don't remember the questions or answers—hopefully St. Peter will be magnanimous—but I remember those ladies and how I wondered if they were happy. I actually had a Sister Michael. This is not her story, but it is the way I would have imagined it.

Thank you for reading and, as ever, I wish you love.

Marie Ferrarella

MARIE FERRARELLA

THE 39-YEAR-OLD VIRGIN

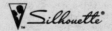

SPECIAL EDITION®

Published by Silhouette Books

America's Publisher of Contemporary Romance

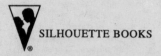 SILHOUETTE BOOKS

ISBN-13: 978-0-373-65465-9

Recycling programs
for this product may
not exist in your area.

THE 39-YEAR-OLD VIRGIN

MARIE FERRARELLA

This *USA TODAY* bestselling and RITA® Award-winning author has written more than one hundred and seventy-five novels for Silhouette Books, some under the name Marie Nicole. Her romances are beloved by fans worldwide. Visit her Web site at www.marieferrarella.com.

To
all the dedicated Dominican Sisters
at
St. Joseph's in Queens, NY,
who passed through
my life

Chapter One

So this nun walks into a popular hot spot...

Ex-nun, Claire corrected herself silently. Dear God, what was she doing here, anyway?

The loud din of voices wedged itself into the throbbing music, forming one large wall of noise that seemed to swirl all around her. Thinking was becoming increasingly more difficult, never mind hearing and talking.

Claire supposed she was daring herself to forge ahead into the life she'd never previously sampled, the life she'd left behind.

Heaven knew that, although popular, she certainly hadn't had more than her share of dates. *Less* would have been a better word to describe the condition of her social life at the time. Her popularity had a universal appeal. She'd been the one people always talked to, the one they wanted to hang out with. She was a "friend" with a capital *F* to all, no matter what gender.

The bottom line was that she'd never had a boyfriend, no steady male in her life to turn to, to nurture secret dreams about. There'd been no one to make her pulse race, her adrenaline flow. She'd never even had a crush, much less been in love.

Was it so wrong to want to discover what she'd missed?

Her fingertips tingled. She was nervous. Just as nervous as she'd been this afternoon when her cousin Nancy, Nancy of the comfortable life, loving husband and four children, had insisted on taking her shopping for not just something suitable to wear tonight, but for undergarments, as well.

"What's wrong with what I have?" she'd asked.

"Nothing, if you want him immediately guessing that you were a nun."

She'd discarded the see-through panties that Nancy held up, trying hard not to blush. "There's not going to be a 'him,'" she insisted.

"Uh-huh." Picking up the panties again, along with two more just like them, Nancy grinned. "On me," she announced, heading toward the register.

Claire wasn't wearing them tonight. No way was she about to sail into a shallow relationship just to make up for lost time. She had to get used to the idea of going out with a man first. And that was going to take time. A lot of time. She'd been a nun for twenty-two years. She'd only been a "civilian" for a couple of weeks. She hadn't even told her mother that she'd left the order permanently when she'd first arrived home. Margaret Santaniello had been under the impression that her only child had gotten a leave of absence in order to care for her during an aggressive bout of leukemia. Her mother, who proudly proclaimed to all who listened that her daughter, Sister Michael, was "married to Jesus," had been horrified when she'd discovered, purely by accident, that Claire, to put it in her mother's words, had "divorced God" because of her.

Her mother had no way of knowing that this turn of events had been a long time in coming. That she hadn't lost her faith, but she had lost her passion. And perhaps lost pieces of herself, as well. Pieces she needed to find again. Pieces that weren't going to turn up here, she thought, looking around at Nancy and the other childhood friends who had dragged her to this place, a restaurant called Saturday Night and Sunday Morning, where "hookups" were the not-so-secret hoped-for outcome of any given evening.

When she'd first thought about leaving the order, when she'd first felt that surge of restlessness, of no longer feeling fulfilled or being on the right track, she'd dreamed of having a family of her own, of children. However, that dream didn't extend to the segment before that ultimate goal was reached. She hadn't thought about dating, or the dreaded step before that—*looking* for a date.

The idea of looking, of actually "dating" terrified her more than going off into the heart of Africa, armed with a truckload of medicine, a crucifix and an untested translator. That she'd undertaken almost fearlessly, believing she had God and right on her side because her intentions were selfless and noble.

God was no longer her copilot. She was flying solo here. And, if examined, her intentions could be deemed as self-centered or self-serving, both foreign feelings to her. The closest she'd come was the notion of remaining alive to see the next sunrise when she and the accompanying nurses had found themselves in enemy territory, caught in cross fire.

She wondered if sitting at a table in Saturday Night and Sunday Morning could be deemed as being stranded in enemy territory.

She would never have come here on her own. But Kelly, Amy and Tess, the three women who had once been so close to her when they were all girls together, and her cousin Nancy had insisted that they come here for her maiden voyage into the secular world.

"Sure you don't want anything stronger than a ginger ale?" Amy asked, fairly shouting the question across the circular table.

In response, Claire wrapped her hand tighter around the tall, slender glass that was now only half-full, holding it as if it were a lifeline to sanity and safety.

"Yes, I'm sure." It wasn't that she'd never had a drink. She could hold her own when it came to hard liquor, like whiskey, something she'd also learned— through necessity—while in Africa, but here she felt she would do far better with a clear head.

Seated at her left side, Kelly leaned in and said the words close to her ear. "You don't look comfortable, Claire."

"I just thought that maybe we could have picked a quieter place to catch up," she answered. "Like the middle of an airport runway."

Amy laughed. "It is kinda noisy, isn't it?"

Nancy, seated on Claire's right, chimed in as she shook her head. It was clear that she considered her cousin her latest project. "There's 'catch up' and then there's 'catch up.'" A wink punctuated the end of her sentence.

Claire had had enough to deal with these last two weeks, getting reacquainted with her mother, finding a routine that suited them both and, come Monday, she was going to be facing a brand new job, presiding over a group of children who would *not* be addressing her as "Sister Michael." With all that going on, she wasn't in the market for, nor had the time for, any male-female relationship. "I don't want to catch up on that just yet."

"You should, Claire. The rest of us have been married at least once, or still are married—" Amy nodded at Nancy "—but you," she said, pointing a scarlet-painted index finger at Claire, "you haven't even gotten your feet wet." She gave her what Claire assumed Amy thought was a penetrating look. "Am I right?"

"I don't think 'feet' are the part of the anatomy that Amy's thinking about," Tess explained. About to say something else, her eyes widened as she zeroed in on someone at the bar. "Now that one's cute," she declared. She squinted, trying to make out someone. "I think I know the guy he's with. Want an introduction?" Tess looked ready to bounce up to her feet at the slightest sign of interest from her.

Claire shook her head vigorously. The last thing she wanted was to have some man dragged over to the table strictly for the purpose of her perusal.

"No, really," she insisted with feeling, grabbing Amy's arm in case the petite blonde was about to run off and make good on her threat. "I just wanted to see my old friends and talk, like we all used to."

"We 'used to' be seventeen and eighteen," Tess told

her. "We're not seventeen and eighteen anymore." She punctuated her statement with a giggle. "Life moves on and all that cr—stuff." She changed the word at the last minute, a guilty expression slipping over her face.

"You can say 'crap' if you want to, Tess. You don't have to temper your language around me," Claire told her. "I'm not Sister Michael anymore."

Tess nodded, as if she should have known that. "Right. Does that mean you can't put in a word with the Big Guy, you know, for your friends?"

Claire smiled, leaning closer in order not to continue shouting. "I can pray for you if that's what you mean, but right now, I'm not too sure if He and I are on the same wavelength."

But she found herself talking to the back of Tess's head. Her friend had turned back around to look toward the bar, to make eye contact with the man she thought she'd recognized.

The latter separated himself from his friend and subsequently made his way over to their table.

Claire watched Tess light up like a desert sunrise, her attention completely riveted on the man who spoke with a slight southern drawl. "Just when I thought I wouldn't be seeing a beautiful lady tonight. Tess, how are you?"

"Just fine. Now," Tess purred.

He nodded toward the incredibly crowded floor just beyond the table. "Would you like to dance?"

Tess was already on her feet and two-thirds of the way into his arms. She took his hand before he had a chance to offer it. "I'd love to."

The next moment, they were swallowed up by the crowd.

It occurred to Claire that their table was located a

few feet shy of what seemed to be the dance floor. A shoe box would have seemed less crowded, she thought.

"Don't worry," Amy said, patting her hand as she, too, began to look around in earnest. "We'll find you someone."

Very gently, Claire drew back her hand. "I don't want someone. I really did come here just to talk."

As she said it, Claire looked accusingly at Nancy, who'd been the first one to contact her with details about the impromptu "get-together." Nancy lifted her shoulders and went through the motions of a helpless shrug, her face the soul of innocence.

Claire wasn't buying it for a minute.

In short order, Amy and then Kelly were whisked away to the dance floor, as well, although Kelly, at least, promised to "be right back."

Claire had her doubts.

As she watched Kelly being led off, she frowned slightly and turned toward Nancy. "Something tells me I should have insisted that we all meet at IHOP."

"Pancakes can't compare to being in the arms of a man," Nancy cracked, then grew serious. "Don't fault them, Claire-bear, they meant well. They also don't think I get out enough," Nancy confided. "This supposedly is as much for me as it is for you."

"But you're married," Claire protested.

"And I make no secret of it." She held up her left hand. Both her wedding ring and her engagement ring were on the appropriate finger. "Patrick doesn't dance and I love to, but you're right, so get rid of that frown."

"I'm not frowning."

"Tell your lips that," Nancy advised. "Besides, once

this latest invader comes along—" she placed her hand on a belly that still had not begun to fill out with its newest occupant despite her being five months along "—I won't be going anywhere for a good long while. This may be my last opportunity to get out."

She supposed she could see her cousin's point. But she still wondered about Nancy's marriage. "Patrick's all right with you coming here?"

"I'm not out trolling for men, Claire-bear," Nancy informed her with a grin. "I'm just here strictly as an observer. Not to mention that he *does* think I've gone to IHOP to meet you."

"Really?"

"No, I'm just kidding." Nancy laughed. "Patrick knows where I am. We have no secrets from each other. And besides," she added seriously, "he trusts me. We trust each other. I guess I'm one of the lucky ones."

Even as she said it, Nancy suddenly looked alert.

Claire scanned the area, expecting to see someone heading their way. But there was no one approaching their table. "What?"

"My phone's vibrating." Nancy pulled the phone out of her pocket. With a finger in one ear, Nancy placed the cell phone against her other one. "Hello? Yes, it's me. Okay, don't worry, it's all right. I'll be right there, honey."

"There?" Claire asked as Nancy shut the phone and put it back in her pocket. "Where's 'there'?"

"Home," Nancy told her. "One of the twins ran into the refrigerator door just as the other one swung it open. She cut her lip," Nancy told her, glancing around the floor for her purse. Locating it, she pulled it up and placed it in front of her on the table. "Patrick gets faint at the sight of blood." She looked apologetic as she added, "I'm sorry to be cutting the evening short."

Claire waved away the apology. This gave her an excuse to leave and she was grateful for it. "That's okay, I think I'm really ready to go."

Nancy looked at her in surprise, then realized the reason for the confusion. "Oh, no, I meant me. You stay, Claire."

Claire said the first thing that came to her head. "You might need a nurse, and I do have a degree, you know."

Nancy stopped for a second and smiled at her even as she shook her head. "I appreciate the offer, Claire, but after four kids, nursing has become second nature to me. Besides, we can't both leave."

"Why not?"

"Because Amy, Tess and Kelly will wonder what happened." Her cousin rose and stood beside her for a second. "Look, I know you're antsy, but just stay a little longer. At least until one of them comes back to the table." She nodded toward the empty chairs. "Until then, you have to guard the purses."

Claire sighed. She'd forgotten about that. "Okay, but the second one of them comes back, I'm leaving."

"Whatever you want," Nancy agreed. "Next time," she promised, "you get to pick the place."

Because she didn't want to detain her cousin any longer, Claire nodded. But there wasn't going to be a "next time." Not for a while, anyway. After one venture, she knew she wasn't ready for this. She needed to get used to the rest of her life first, get comfortable in her responsibilities and new routine. Then—maybe—she'd *think* about going to a place like Saturday Night and Sunday Morning to meet men.

And then again, maybe not.

Claire looked at Nancy as the latter pushed her chair in. "Give me a call and tell me how she's doing when you get a chance."

Clutching her purse, Nancy leaned over the table and gave her hand a squeeze. "Will do. And try to have a good time while you're still here."

Claire forced a smile to her lips. "I'll do my best."

"Do better," Nancy instructed, then hurried off. And Claire felt very alone.

How long did these songs last, anyway? she wondered impatiently. Wasn't it about time at least one of the girls came back?

"Looks like all your friends deserted you, little lady."

Despite the noise, Claire heard the words clearly. Startled, she swung around and discovered a tall man standing directly behind her chair. And he was looking right at her.

"Not quite," she replied. "Three of them are on the floor, dancing. My cousin had to leave."

"Lucky for me." He was good-looking in a non-rugged, stockbroker kind of way. If she were to judge, she would have put him in his early forties. You'd think after all that time, he would have learned not to go where he wasn't invited. But instead, he dropped down into the seat beside her.

Nancy's seat, she thought grudgingly. "So, what's your name, pretty lady?"

"Claire," she heard herself saying even though she had a feeling that she should have given him a false name, or, even better, none at all.

"Claire," he repeated, nodding his approval. "Nice change from 'Tiffany' and 'Britney,'" he commented.

Putting out his hand, he grinned broadly. She couldn't get the image of a shark out of her head. "I'm Bill."

Not shaking his hand would have been rude and she didn't want to be rude, so she shook it with no enthusiasm and murmured, "Hello, Bill."

He kept his hand around hers. "I like the way you say that."

Very deliberately, she withdrew her hand from his. "Look, I don't want you to get the wrong idea. I'm not here to mingle."

"Oh?" Rather than put off, he seemed pleased. Before she realized what he was doing, he ran the back of his knuckles slowly against her cheek. Stiffening, Claire immediately pulled her head back. "A lady who wants to cut to the chase right off the bat. I like that."

"I'm not here to 'cut to the chase,'" she informed him. "I'm here with my friends to do a little catching up."

Instead of backing away, Bill took hold of her wrist and then rose, pulling her up to her feet with him. "Why don't we teach your friends a lesson and have them come looking for you? My car's right outside."

Obviously, the man refused to take a hint. There was no way she was about to go anywhere with this man. But she still tried to be polite. "No, thank you, I'd rather not."

A flash of anger came and went from the dark eyes. His grip on her wrist tightened. "Don't be a tease, Claire. Men don't like that."

She glared at him. Fear had left, replaced by anger. "And I don't like being manhandled."

"What are you, one of them?" he asked contemptuously.

She knew where he was going. It might be easier just to agree, to let him think her preference ran toward the softer gender, but that would have been an out-and-out lie. She preferred a shade of gray instead.

"What I am," she informed him, tossing her head, "is a nun." *God forgive me for lying.*

"A nun, huh?" The news did not have the desired effect on the man. Rather than release her and mumble an apology, Bill leered at her as he let his gaze travel over the length of her and then back up. "Never had a nun before." His hand tightened even more around her wrist and he pulled her toward him. "Now you've really piqued my interest. C'mon, dance with me, 'Sister' Claire. Show me what you've got." The leer deepened. "I bet you're really starved for a little action."

So much for being polite, she thought. "If I were, it wouldn't be with such a Neanderthal," she declared, trying in vain to pull back. She was no weakling, but he was far too strong for her.

"Not the right answer." The warning came out like a half growl.

"But it's the one you're going to accept," someone said directly behind her. "Now."

Chapter Two

Caleb McClain ran his fingers along the chunky shot glass sitting on the slick bar before him.

He knew he should be on his way.

Hell, he wasn't even sure what had made him stop here at Saturday's rather than simply going to Lucky's, the bar located near the precinct.

Maybe it was because he wanted the excuse of going to a restaurant rather than a bar. More likely, it was because he didn't want to run into anyone from the station. Tonight of all nights, he didn't feel like talking. Not that anyone would expect him to be talkative. Never one to shoot the breeze, the way his partner, Mark Falkowski, did, he'd become one step removed from being a mummy in the last year.

At least that was what Falkowski maintained. Ski was the only man who would attempt to broach the subject that had so viciously scarred him and even the six-foot-six vice detective didn't venture very far into that territory. Ski knew better. *Everyone* knew better. Just like everyone knew the reason why he'd withdrawn so completely into himself.

One year. One year today.

How the hell did time go by so fast when it felt like it was standing still, when every second of every day seemed to pierce him with sharpened spears?

And today was the worst of all. Today marked 365 days since it'd happened. Since Ski had come to him with a long face and sorrow in his eyes to tell him what the beat cops in East L.A. had just called in.

Getting out of bed today had been almost impossible. He'd thought of calling in sick, but where would he go, what would he do? Everywhere he went, his mind went with him.

There was no escape.

Staying in the house wasn't the answer. Danny would be there. He didn't want his son seeing him like this. The boy needed to be shielded, but he couldn't pretend that he was all right. He could pull it off for short periods of time. But not today.

The mere thought of his wife had his throat threatening to close up on him. Whatever air was left in his lungs wasn't enough.

Jane.

Jane, with her bright, eager smile, her desire to put a bandage on the whole world and somehow make it all better through sheer force of will and her infinite capacity to love.

Anger surged, channeling itself through his hand. His fingers tightened around the glass so hard, he realized that he'd wind up shattering it. Loosening his hold took effort. Effort not to go over the edge. Every day was a struggle.

If it hadn't been for that Mother Teresa attitude of hers, her determination to boldly go where even angels had better sense than to tread, Jane would still be alive today. Alive instead of a victim of the mindless feuding of two rival gangs. She was there, about to get into her car, when the shooting started. Caught in the cross fire, she was one of several people to die that afternoon.

The only one who'd mattered to him.

A year ago. Exactly one year ago today, her young, beautiful life had been senselessly cut short because she had to go see the pregnant girl who was one of the cases she handled as a social worker. The girl was sixteen and already the mother of two. He'd told Jane she was wasting her time, but Jane had been convinced she could turn the girl around, help her get her life together.

She could be so stubborn when she wanted to be. He'd begged her to take a different job, to be reassigned, or, even better, just stay home and be Danny's mother and his wife and make them both supremely happy. But Jane had to be Jane. She was determined to save the world, one lost soul at a time. So she went.

And instead of saving that pregnant girl, Jane had lost her life that day and he, he'd lost his main reason for living. Nothing else seemed to really matter to him, even though he kept trying to go through the motions. He continued being a cop because that was all he knew and he had to do something to pay the bills and keep a roof over Danny's head.

He shouldn't feel this way. Jane wouldn't want him

to be like this and it was because of Danny that he hadn't pulled the trigger of the gun he'd cradled in his lap night after night that first week, raising it to his lips time and again, desperate for oblivion.

But that would have left Danny an orphan and he couldn't do that to the boy. It wouldn't have been fair to deprive him of a father after he'd lost his mother. So he'd put the gun down and stayed alive. In a manner of speaking.

Instead of killing himself, in order to survive, to deal with the huge waves of pain that would wash over him without warning, he'd gone numb. Absolutely and completely numb.

A twinge would break through, every now and then, and Caleb would tell himself that he'd try. Try to break out of his invisible prison and be emotionally available to his son. But every time he did, the pain would find him, oppressing him to the point that he was no good to anyone. So he retreated, telling Danny he'd make it up to him later. And the boy forgave him, each and every time.

I'm sorry, Danny. I really am.

Caleb looked at his near-empty glass. He debated getting another drink. The raw whiskey went down much too easily. But it made no difference. One or ten, the result was the same. Nothing really blotted out the pain and he had to drive home. Killing himself was one thing, but possibly killing someone else, someone who had nothing to do with the tragedy that haunted him, was something he wasn't willing to risk.

Besides, Mrs. Collins had a home to go to. She'd already been there longer than agreed upon. Edna Collins was a godsend who lived in the single-story house across the street. The widowed grandmother was more than happy to watch Danny for him after school and whenever his work took him away. It gave her something to do, she'd told him. She hadn't even wanted payment for her time, but he'd persuaded her to take it.

Tilting his glass, Caleb stared down at the bottom. The amber liquid was all gone except for what amounted to one last drop. Despite his earlier resolve, he debated getting just one more before he hit the road and went home.

Caleb really wasn't sure just what had made him look in the direction that he did. Over at one of the tables, a woman tried to fend off the advances of some would-be Romeo who didn't look as if he liked taking "no" for an answer. Well, what the hell did she expect, coming to a place like this?

He was about to look away, when something nudged at a vague, faraway place in his brain. A memory tried to break through.

Something about the torrent of red hair, the way she tossed her head, seemed familiar to him.

Remembering was just out of reach.

Did he know her?

Probably not. Maybe she just resembled someone he'd dealt with. God knew he came across so many people in his line of work....

Caleb looked closer.

And then he remembered.

Or thought he did. Curious, he decided it bore investigation. But for that, he needed to get closer. Setting down his glass, he tossed a tip onto the counter.

The next moment, he was striding across the

crowded floor, carelessly moving aside anyone and everyone in his way with less regard than if they'd been cardboard placeholders.

The closer he got, the surer he became. And yet, it hardly seemed possible.

But it was, wasn't it? he silently asked that part of his mind that still retained a few less damaged memories, memories that had been gathered before Jane had entered his life.

And before she'd left it.

Red hair, skin like alabaster. Green eyes. Delicate-looking.

It was Claire Santaniello.

No one else had hair quite that shade of red. Confusion snaked its way through him at the same time that a tiny microchip of warmth made its appearance.

Damn, what was she doing here in a place like this?

Assessing the situation with lightning speed, he told the other man to back away. The expression in the other man's eyes was pure malevolence as he looked away from Claire and at him.

"You want her for yourself?" the other man growled, holding on to Claire's wrist as firmly as a handcuff. "Tough. I was here first."

This was absurd. Never in her wildest dreams had she *ever* conceived of this kind of scenario. Served her right for not standing her ground and leaving the moment she realized what sort of place the girls were bringing her to.

"Nobody was 'first,'" Claire snapped, losing her patience. "I'm not some bone you two can scrap over. I'm not interested. In *anybody*," she declared with finality just in case the man who'd just come to her so-called rescue had any ideas about the "winner getting the spoils" once he got rid of Neanderthal Man.

It was Claire, all right, Caleb thought. He was sure of it. "You heard the lady," he said evenly. "She wants you to go." It wasn't a statement, it was an order.

The other man obviously saw it as more of a challenge. "You gonna make me?"

"Why don't you step up to the plate and see?" Caleb's voice took on a sort of deadly calm. He deliberately moved so that the other man could see the holstered gun strapped on beneath the navy sport jacket.

His eyes fastened on the weapon, Claire's would-be lover sucked in his breath. He let loose a scathing curse before abandoning the virtual tug-of-war.

"She's probably frigid," he threw in with contempt. "You're welcome to her." With that, he turned away and melted into the crowd.

Squaring her shoulders, Claire turned around to get a good look at the man who had come to her aid. She was torn between thinking that chivalry wasn't dead and wondering if she'd just gone from the frying pan into the fire.

Most of all, she didn't want this new contestant in the battle of the dance floor thinking that she was some kind of defenseless weakling. She'd stood up to more dangerous men than the one who'd just left. Of course, that had been when she and God had been on speaking terms.

Was this some guardian angel He'd sent in His place? She would have liked to think so, but she had a feeling that wasn't the case. "Thank you, but I could have handled him."

"No, you couldn't," Caleb said matter-of-factly.

There wasn't a hint of amusement in his voice, but neither was there any annoyance. "He had at least a hundred pounds on you." He paused, then added, "He's not a little boy you can just send off to bed because it's past his bedtime."

The voice was deep and slightly gravelly. There was no reason for it to be familiar, and yet, the cadence managed to rustle a deep, faraway corner of her mind.

Did she know him? Was he someone she'd gone to school with? The lighting was far from good, designed more for seduction and to hide imperfections than to highlight anything. Claire squinted, studying the rugged, chiseled face, the somber yet ever so slightly amused expression beginning to emerge. Her eyes shifted to his sandy-blond hair and light blue eyes.

He didn't look familiar, but that didn't take away from the fact that he somehow *seemed* familiar. She wasn't about to ask "Do I know you?" because even she knew that would sound like a line and it might very well open an undesirable door.

And then the familiar stranger stopped being a stranger with his very next words.

"What's the matter, Claire?" he asked. "Don't you remember me?"

She stood there, trapped in a memory that refused to gel even if it did produce flashes in her head. "You know my name."

"I know a lot of things about you," he told her, his amusement growing. "I know you used to like to watch detective shows, but that you wouldn't if you had any homework to do. You did it first, then watched. I know you used to sing to yourself when you were studying when you thought no one was around to hear you."

Her mouth dropped open as she stared at the tall man before her. She should know him, she realized, and yet, no name rose to her lips. "Who are you?"

Caleb had no idea why he didn't answer her question directly, why he didn't just tell her his name instead of choosing to prolong the mystery for her just a little longer. He nodded at the table, indicating that she take a seat, then, switching it around, he straddled a chair himself. He watched her sink down into the nearest one as if she intended to shoot up to her feet at any second.

"Who do you think I am?" he asked her.

Claire stared at him intently, her green eyes sweeping over him. When he'd stood behind her and she'd turned around, she'd noted that he was almost a foot taller than she was. The man had shoulders like a football guard and it wasn't thanks to any padding in his jacket. She could tell by the way he moved.

"Possibly what I'd imagined my guardian angel looked like," she answered, her mouth curving slightly, "but then if you were my guardian angel, that Neanderthal wouldn't have been able to see you."

For a glimmer of a moment, he was back in the past. The past where anything was possible and the blinding hurt hadn't found him yet. Caleb decided to give her another clue.

"I became a cop because of all those detective shows you used to watch. You didn't know it, but I used to sneak out of my room and watch them with you. I'd sit on the top step, just outside my bedroom door, and watch the show—when I wasn't watching you," he added. Then, for the first time in a very long time, he allowed himself a genuine smile. "I had one hell of a crush on you, Claire."

He said her name as if they were old friends. So why couldn't she remember him?

Who *was* he?

"I still don't—" And then her eyes widened as she processed what he'd just told her. The connection came to her riding a lightning bolt. "Caleb? Caleb Mc-Clain?" she cried, not completely convinced that she was right.

But it was the only answer that made any sense, given what he'd just told her. He was the only little boy she used to babysit. Except that he wasn't little anymore. And definitely not a boy.

My God, she felt old.

Caleb nodded. "It's Detective McClain now."

Even though she'd guessed right, Claire could hardly believe it. Except for the color of his eyes—electric blue—and his hair—a dark sandy-blond—he bore no resemblance to the small, wiry, semishy little boy she used to babysit on a regular basis.

"How long has it been?" she heard herself asking, raising her voice as the music grew louder again.

Caleb brought his chair in closer. "Twenty-two years. Ever since you went off to that convent in New York."

She'd broken his heart that summer. Up until that time, he'd been nursing his crush, thinking it love, and making plans for the two of them and their future together once he gained a few inches on her. The fact that he was five years younger had never fazed him in the slightest. As an only child, he'd always felt older than he was.

Caleb frowned slightly as he regarded her. She was dressed conservatively enough, certainly not like most of the women here. In a two-piece cream-colored suit with the hint of a rose blouse peeking out, she looked more like she was on her way to a board meeting than a place where singles converged and mingled.

It didn't make sense, her being here like this. "Do they encourage nuns to frequent places like this?" he asked. "Are you on some mission, looking for converts?"

She was seriously thinking of having cards printed up with a disclaimer written across them. It would certainly save time. "I'm not part of the Dominican Sisters anymore."

"What happened? I heard my parents talking about your decision to join an order. My mother said you had the calling." He didn't add that he felt his heart was going to break that entire summer. Those were merely the thoughts of a highly impressionable twelve-year-old.

Real heartbreak, he now knew, was so much harder to survive.

Claire shrugged, falling back on the excuse she'd given her mother because it was the only simple way she could summarize what had happened. "My 'calling' just stopped calling."

Outside the job, he never prodded. Everyone had a right to their privacy. Still, because this was Claire, the "woman" from his childhood, something kept him in the chair, talking. "So, are you just passing through?"

"No, I'm staying. For now." Why she felt it was necessary to qualify her words, she wasn't sure. Maybe because she felt so uncertain about what to do with this new life. "My mother's ill—" a nice safe word for what was wrong, she thought "—and right now, she needs someone to be there for her." Although, she added silently, her mother was still almost every bit as feisty as she used to be and determined to keep her independence. If she hadn't gotten a copy of the lab report, she would never have guessed that there was anything wrong with her mother except a bout of fatigue.

He caught himself vaguely wondering what this mysterious malady was, but he left it alone. Wasn't any of his business. "I'm sorry to hear that."

She nodded in response to the sentiment he'd expressed. "Thank you. In the meantime, I've just gotten a job at an elementary school." A job. It still felt rather odd to say that. She'd been a Dominican Sister for so long, being anything else was going to take a great deal of adjustment. But they were going to need the money, now that her mother had retired. And there might come a time when her mother would need around-the-clock care, so she needed to amass a nest egg now. "I start next week."

He could see her as a teacher, he thought. "Which school?"

"Lakewood Elementary." Caleb laughed shortly under his breath. It wasn't a response she would have anticipated. "What?"

"Nothing." But the expression on her face prodded him to elaborate. "It's just that it's a small world." There were a total of six elementary schools in Bedford. It seemed ironic that she should get a job at this one. "That's the school my son goes to."

A son. The boy she'd babysat had a son. Sometimes she forgot that other people went on to have lives while she'd been sequestered in tiny villages where running water was considered a luxury.

Claire smiled. "You have a son."

Her whole face still lit up when she smiled, Caleb noted. That was what had first captured his preadolescent heart, her smile. It surprised him to discover that there were some things that *hadn't* changed.

"Yeah," he finally acknowledged. "I've got a son."

Obviously, he wasn't one of those fathers who liked to brag, she thought. "What's his name?"

"Danny."

Definitely not in the bragging league. "Do you have a picture of him?" she coaxed.

He did, but the one he carried in his wallet was a two-year-old-photograph of both Danny and Jane. Right now, he didn't feel up to seeing it. So he lied.

"No, not on me." He really had to get going. And yet, somehow, he continued to remain straddling the chair, his arms crossed over the back, just looking at her. He'd never expected to see her again. "If you don't mind my asking," he began in his gruff detective's voice, then tempered it as he continued, "what are you doing in a place like this?"

"I was asking myself the same question. Some of my friends talked me into coming here with them. I think this is their way of 'breaking me in.'"

"And where are they now?"

"One, my cousin Nancy, had to leave," she explained. "The other three—" she waved a vague hand toward the throng "—are out there somewhere on the floor."

Presumably not alone, Caleb surmised. He rose from the chair and pushed it back toward the table. "Well, I've got to get going." But his feet still weren't moving. And he knew why. He felt as if he was deserting her, leaving her to be preyed on by the next over-sexed male. Which was why, he supposed, the next minute he heard himself asking, "You want a ride home?"

Claire popped up to her feet as if she'd been launched by a catapult, crying "Yes" with such enthusiasm and relief he found it difficult not to laugh.

Placing a hand to the small of her back, he urged, "Then c'mon."

Chapter Three

But instead of heading for the door the way he'd expected her to, Claire asked him to indulge her for a moment.

It occurred to Caleb that, up to this point, he'd actually been talking to the Claire from his past. Twenty-two years did a lot to change a person and he really didn't know the woman beside him at all, just who she had been.

"Exactly what do you have in mind?" he wanted to know.

"It won't take long, I promise," she told him. As she spoke, she carelessly placed a hand to his chest, as if to hold him in place. She was a toucher, he remembered. It was one of the things that had set his young heart pounding and his mind spinning romantic scenarios. God, had he *ever* really been that young? "Wait right here."

Puzzled, he did as she asked. He had no idea what was on her mind until he saw her burrow her way into the throng and corner a vivacious-looking brunette. The latter's abbreviated dress appeared to be half a size too small in all possible directions.

The next moment, she was edging the woman out of the crowd. Bringing her back to the table. Trailing after the woman, looking mildly interested, was the man who'd just been gyrating with the brunette on the dance floor.

"Kelly, you have to watch the purses," Claire told her friend. "Nancy got an emergency call so she went home, and I'm leaving."

The woman referred to as Kelly looked past Claire and directly at him. The grin on the brunette's face was so wide Caleb suspected he could have driven a squad car through it without touching either corner.

"You got lucky," Kelly cried with triumphant glee, the man standing behind her temporarily forgotten. "First time out, too."

"Yes, I got lucky," Claire responded. "Because I ran into an old friend. He's taking me home."

The moment she said it, referring to Caleb as a friend, it felt a little odd. She'd never thought of him that way before. The last time she'd seen him, he had been wearing pajamas embossed with figures from a Saturday-morning cartoon show and his head had barely reached her chin. Short for his age, the boy she remembered bore next to no resemblance to the man standing by her right now. This man all but reeked of quiet self-confidence. And masculinity.

"I should have old friends like that," Kelly murmured, her eyes sweeping over him appreciatively.

"Go, don't worry about anything." She leaned into Claire. "Purses would be the last thing on my mind if I were going home with someone like that."

Claire shook her head. Obviously, Kelly was going to think what she wanted to think. "G'night, Kelly," she said, turning away from the table.

"Ready?" Caleb asked patiently.

"Absolutely." She'd had enough of this kind of singles' club to last a lifetime.

"Be gentle with her," Kelly called after them.

When Caleb turned around to look at the brunette, she winked at him. Not flirtatiously, but as if he and she were privy to some shared secret.

Noting the wink, Claire picked up her pace, weaving her way to the front entrance.

The moment they stepped outside and the door closed behind them, Claire paused to take in a deep breath, savoring the cool air. It had been hot and stuffy inside; all those bodies packed into such a small space had generated a lot of heat.

She savored the quiet even more. The old line about not being able to hear herself think ran through her head. There was a great deal of truth in that, Claire mused.

And then she looked at Caleb. She was rather good at reading body language. His said he was running low on patience. Nodding off toward the left, he began walking.

"I'm sorry about Kelly," she told him.

His hand lightly pressing the small of her back, Caleb guided her toward the side parking lot. As far as he knew, she hadn't done anything annoying or offensive. "What are you sorry about?"

"Kelly views any male over the age of eighteen as fair game." It felt awkward, talking about dating with him, even nebulously. That in itself felt strange. She'd never had trouble talking about anything before. She'd lost count of all the times she'd answered shy, misguided questions about sex from adolescents who hadn't a clue about what was going on with them.

Well, she'd started this, she had to finish it. Gracefully, if possible. "Kelly seems to think I have to make up for lost time and I think she pegged you as my initiator."

He stopped walking and looked at Claire. She'd lost him. "Initiator for…?"

She put it in as formal terms as she could. "My entrance into the world of romantic liaisons." Caleb was shaking his head. Again, there was just the barest whisper of a smile on his lips. The Caleb she remembered was always grinning. What had changed that? she wondered. "What?"

He directed her over to his Mercury sedan, digging into the front pocket of his jeans for the key.

"You still talk flowery. I used to like listening to you talk, even when I didn't have a clue what you were talking about. It sounded pretty." The truth of it was, he loved the sound of her voice. He used to pray his parents would go out for the evening so that she would come over and babysit him. Or, as she had referred to it, "young man sit" with him. Looking back, he realized that she was always careful not to bruise his young ego. "I thought that maybe you were going to be a writer or something."

That occupation had merited about five minutes of consideration before she'd discarded the idea. "I liked to read more than I liked to write, so I opted to become 'or something.'"

Caleb unlocked the passenger-side door and then held it open for her. The thought that she had certainly become "something" whispered across his mind. "I always wondered, why a convent?"

Getting in, Claire buckled up, then sat back in the seat. She tried to relax, but some of the residual tension refused to leave her body.

"Lots of reasons, I guess. They all seemed very viable at the time." She'd wanted to serve God and help humanity. Did that sound as hopelessly idealistic as she thought it did? She glanced at Caleb as he got in behind the steering wheel. "But they're all behind me now."

He knew she was saying she didn't want to talk about it, that the subject was private. He could more than relate to that even though a part of him remained curious.

"Fair enough," he allowed. "So you're going to teach, huh?"

"Yes. I'm a little nervous," she admitted freely. "But I am really looking forward to it." The last class she'd taught was more than a year ago and it had been halfway around the world. They had been happy to get anyone. She considered herself lucky that the school here had accepted her. "I've always liked kids—and I'd like to think they like me."

Leaving the parking lot, he nodded. "They probably do," he said matter-of-factly.

Claire grinned. "And you know this for a fact."

He surprised her by giving her a serious answer. "You don't talk down to them," he told her. "That's what I liked about you." One of many, many things, but he didn't add that. The thoughts of a preadolescent boy belonged in the past. "You didn't make me feel like some dumb little kid you could boss around."

Never once did she lord it over him, even though he knew that he would have willingly submitted to her authority, just to have her there.

"That's because you weren't some dumb little kid," she pointed out. "You were very smart—even if you pretended not to be." His eyebrows narrowed in a quizzical glance he sent her way. "All those homework problems you used to ask me to help you with," she recalled for his benefit. "I knew you could do them on your own."

He'd forgotten about that. Forgotten a lot about his earlier life, the way things were when he was growing up and believed the world held so much promise. "What gave me away?"

"You 'caught on' much too quickly when I helped you with your math homework. You would have had to have understood the principle to some extent for that to have happened." She smiled at him fondly, remembering evenings in the kitchen with books spread out, his and hers. She'd thought of him as the little brother she hadn't been allowed to have. Michael, who had died long before he was a year old. "I think you were trapped between wanting me to spend time with you, helping you with your homework, and struggling to keep from trying to impress me with how bright you really were."

He laughed quietly to himself. She'd hit the nail dead on its head. "You shouldn't have become a nun, you should have become a detective."

"I'll keep that in mind as a backup career if teaching and nursing don't pan out."

He took a left turn at the end of the next long block, passing by a newly constructed strip mall. "You're a nurse, too?"

She nodded. The order she'd joined had specifically encouraged her educational pursuits. "I thought getting a nursing degree would come in handy in the places that the order kept sending me to."

"And that was?"

She rattled off the names of several small countries, some of which had already changed their name again. "Africa, for the most part," she added, since that was the easiest way to keep track.

He could have easily made the yellow light up ahead before it turned red, but instead, he eased his foot off the gas pedal, switching to the brake. The vehicle slowly came to a stop.

The moment that it did, Caleb turned to look at her in sheer awe, her words playing themselves over in his head. Try as he might, he couldn't picture her braving the elements, going from village to village, dispensing hope and medicine. It was difficult enough picturing her in the traditional garb of a Dominican Sister, swaddled from head to foot in black with white contrasts and roasting beneath the hot, merciless sun.

He couldn't have explained why, but he was suddenly glad that was all behind her.

Very little really surprised him. Somewhere along the line, between his work and Jane's death, he'd lost the ability to be amazed. But this came close.

"You went to Africa?" he finally asked. "On your own?"

Being in Africa for all those long periods of time

had a great deal to do with who she'd been and who she had become. "Yes, why?"

He shrugged. The light turned green and they continued on their way. "I just thought you were in some cloistered place, far away from everyone." Like Rapunzel in the tower, he remembered thinking. He'd been baptized Catholic at birth, but neither he nor his parents before him had ever really taken an active part in any organized religion. And Jane had been a free spirit, embracing everything, singling out nothing. His image of what nuns actually did was very limited. "Fingering your beads and praying."

Someone else might have taken offense at the near flippant way he regarded those who had dedicated themselves to the religious life, but she knew he didn't mean to sound belittling. Something else was going on, something he tried to keep buried. Maybe it had to do with his line of work. She'd known more than one burned-out police officer.

"Praying was a large part of it," she acknowledged, "but God helps those who help themselves. In my case, I was the one doing the helping."

"In Africa," he repeated, the slightest trace of wonder creeping into his voice.

"That's right."

Caleb thought about some of the articles he'd read in the newspaper and heard on the news over the years. Stories about wars between African factions and atrocities that were committed. "Were you ever in any danger?"

She inclined her head. "At times." Her tone made light of the admission. She'd never been the type to seek the spotlight for its own sake, only as a necessary evil when focusing on raising funds to buy the simplest of supplies for the villages she went to. "One of the biggest dangers I faced was finding someplace to wash that didn't have a hippo in it. They're not the docile creatures everyone thinks they are. They can get pretty nasty. Makes you see the world in a different light and makes you truly grateful for the simplest modern convenience." She grinned. "Like toilet paper."

He listened quietly. When she paused, he commented, "I can see why you'd want to leave that."

He'd misunderstood her meaning, she thought. "I never minded the harsh conditions. It was a small price to pay for being able to help people, to do some good for those less fortunate. Some of the things I've seen could break your heart," she said with a heartfelt sigh. "I might even opt to go back someday."

He frowned. Was she having a change of heart? "Then you think you'll reenlist?"

"Reenlist?" she echoed, amused by the term.

He made a sharp left. She caught herself leaning into him. "As a nun."

"Anything's possible," she allowed. "But at this point, I don't really think I'm going to 'reenlist' in the order. Besides, my being part of a religious order was neither a plus nor a minus when it came to the work I was doing in Africa. I can just as easily go back there as a civilian."

In some ways, she added silently, it might even be easier that way. They wouldn't be turning to her, expecting answers to the questions that troubled their souls. Because she didn't feel as if she had the answers any longer. If anything, she shared their questions.

"Do you want to?" he asked bluntly.

Claire pressed her lips together, suppressing a sigh as Caleb drove down the street that led to the far-side entrance to her development.

"I'm not sure what I want right now," Claire told him honestly. "Other than doing whatever's necessary to make sure my mother gets well."

"What does she have?"

The word all but burned on her tongue as she said it. "She has acute leukemia. It seems that she's had it for a while now, but I just found out recently."

He wasn't all that familiar with the ramifications of the disease, but he knew it wasn't anything good. "I'm sorry."

She appreciated his sentiment, but she wasn't going to let dark thoughts get the better of her. She was here to raise her mother's spirits and do anything else she could for her, not to let her own spirits drag her down.

"It's not necessarily a death sentence," she told him. She'd done her homework. "There've been plenty of people who have had long remissions."

He made another right turn, slowing his pace down to twenty miles an hour, then spared her a glance. "You're still an optimist, even after working in third-world countries?"

Despite working in third-world countries, she corrected silently.

Working in Africa was what had started the ball rolling to her ultimately leaving the order. Ever since she'd been a child she'd been taught that God wasn't to be questioned, that His ways weren't to be measured by the same rules as those that were applied to the people He'd created.

But, try as she might, she just couldn't help herself.

Couldn't completely lock away the horror and the feeling of disappointment she'd experienced, and kept experiencing, whenever she thought of all the children who had died of the plague in that one village. All the children she hadn't been able to help.

She'd been sent there, she'd really believed, to act as an instrument of God—and still she couldn't save them, couldn't help.

Because He hadn't helped.

These were all thoughts she couldn't voice, couldn't even find any relief by talking about to the people who could give her some insight into the matter. She knew she would be told she was being blasphemous. And maybe she was, but she couldn't just accept that, in some way, God couldn't be held accountable for all those young lives that had been cut so short.

Caleb glanced at her again and she realized that he was waiting for her to say something.

"Not as much of an optimist as I once was," she finally replied, saying each word carefully.

"But you still are one," he pointed out.

She supposed that was what kept her going, what made her still think that what she did made a difference in the grand scheme of things. "Yes."

"Why?"

The single word was razor sharp. Was he challenging her? Or was he somehow asking her to give him an explanation so that he could find his way to optimism himself?

She did her best to make him understand. "Because without optimism, we can't go on. Optimism is just hope dressed up in formal clothes. And without hope, the soul has nothing to cling to, the spirit dies."

Caleb laughed shortly. "Yeah, tell me about it."

Claire eyed this familiar stranger who'd reentered her life after all these years. His profile had gone rigid, as if he'd suddenly realized he'd just let something slip that wasn't supposed to be exposed. Her need·to help, to comfort, to make things better, surfaced instantly.

"Maybe you can tell me," she coaxed.

"Sisters can hear confessions now?" Caleb said to her flippantly.

"Is it something you need to confess, Caleb?" she asked gently.

This was getting far too personal. He didn't want her digging around in his life, even if her intentions were altruistic. "Just a play on words, Claire. I don't have anything to confess."

She regarded him for a long moment. "That would make you a minority of one."

"No, just someone who doesn't believe." He squinted slightly as he tried to make out a street sign. This was the old development. He'd grown up here, but it had been a long time since he'd been back. His parents had moved shortly after Claire had left to join the order and he had had no reason to return.

"In confession?" she asked, although she had a feeling that his meaning was broader.

The next moment, her fears were confirmed. "In anything."

There was loneliness in his words, whether he knew it or not. It horrified her that Caleb felt so alone, so adrift. But telling him that would only make things worse.

Still, she didn't want to just drop the subject, either, so she tried to make light of it and hope that he'd wind up wanting to talk. "Well, that certainly is a sweeping statement."

Where was all this coming from? He didn't usually talk, much less open parts of himself up. Had to be because of what day it was, he thought.

I miss you, Jane. "Sorry, didn't mean to get this serious."

She hated to see any creature in pain, she always had. "If you ever want to talk, you know where to find me."

"I don't," Caleb told her sharply. "Want to talk," he clarified. "There's nothing to talk about." Pressing down on the gas pedal, he made short work of the last half block. "We're here," he announced.

Pulling up in the driveway beside the vintage vehicle her father had left her mother, he put his car into Park, but didn't turn off the ignition. The car continued to hum quietly, like a tamed cheetah, waiting for the time it could stretch its legs again.

Claire got out of the car. She sensed that he wanted to make a quick getaway. Even so, she asked, "Would you like to come in for some coffee?"

Despite his desire to escape, he was tempted. For old-times' sake. But he knew it was for the best if he just got going. So he shook his head. "I'm already pretty late."

So he'd mentioned earlier, she thought. "Right. I'm sorry, I'm keeping you from your son and your wife."

His expression darkened for a moment, as if something painful had gripped him in its claws, but he made no comment other than "G'night."

The next second, he was pulling out of her driveway and speeding away.

Chapter Four

"So you're really going through with it."

Looking up from the bureau, Claire saw her mother standing in the doorway of her room. In a hurry to get ready and out the door, and more than a little anxious about her first day at Lakewood Elementary, she hadn't heard her mother until she was almost inside the room.

Claire's eyes met her mother's in the mirror. "'It?'"

Margaret nodded as she walked across the threshold. Gone were the trim business suits she used to favor. She'd slipped on aqua-colored sweatpants and a matching sweatshirt, both of which provided a vivid contrast to the rich red hair she's always been so proud of.

She didn't look like a woman who was ill, Claire thought. Maybe God still had one miracle left with her name on it after all. Mentally, she crossed her fingers.

"You know." Margaret frowned as if the very word she was about to utter tasted bitter. "Teaching."

Claire was somewhat surprised that, when she woke up this morning after a not-so-restful night, she was in the grip of first-day jitters. She supposed it had something to do with wanting validation for the decision she'd made about the new direction of her life. Whatever the reason, the jitters were worse than she'd expected and her mother's disapproving expression wasn't exactly helping.

She glanced at her mother over her shoulder. "Yes, Mother," she replied patiently. "I'm really going through with it. In approximately—" she glanced at her watch, "—an hour and ten minutes, I'll be taking over what would have been Mrs. Butterfield's fourth-grade class if she wasn't about to deliver at any minute."

Claire turned back toward the mirror to check over her appearance one last time. And perhaps locate her confidence, as well.

Margaret sighed and shook her head. "Why are you doing this?"

At the last moment, Claire had decided to wear her hair up. She thought it looked more authoritative that way. Besides, to be honest, she wasn't all that accustomed to seeing her hair loose like this. Swiftly, she began to strategically place pins in it to ensure that it stayed in place.

"Because, for one thing, I need a job." *And we're going to need the money, Mom,* she added silently.

"No, you don't," her mother contradicted. "You already have a job."

The last pin in, Claire quickly surveyed her handiwork. "You mean taking care of you—" Was her mother trying to tell her that she felt weak? That she needed her around in case she suddenly began to go downhill?

But before she got a chance to ask, her mother had already waved a dismissive hand at her, silencing any words that were about to emerge. "No, I can take care of myself, Claire," she declared with dignity. "I'm not an invalid—at least, not yet," she qualified quietly.

Finished, Claire turned away from the bureau. This was as good as it was going to get, she thought. Worrying about the way her hair looked and if her clothes were sending the wrong message was an entirely foreign concept to her. So was experimenting with makeup, but she felt she'd done a fairly admirable job of it for someone new to the game. The application was subtle, the results pretty.

The next second, she admonished herself for being vain. It was hard being stuck between two worlds, not feeling as if she belonged in either.

"Then I don't know what you're—"

Again her mother cut her short, this time with more than a trace of impatience. "Your job. Your vocation." The frown mingled with a plea. "I'm talking about your being part of the Dominican order."

Not now, Mother. Not today, please.

She'd known the moment the idea of leaving the order had occurred to her that the transition wasn't going to be easy. For either of them. Not for her because she'd been part of the order for so long, she was going to have a difficult time redefining herself in different terms, and not for her widowed mother because she knew that Margaret Santaniello was convinced that turning her back on the order was tantamount to committing a mortal sin and thus putting her soul in jeopardy.

Getting her mother to come around would require treating both the subject and her mother with kid gloves. And, she'd already learned, it was also going to require a great deal of repetition.

She tried to focus on another time, a time when she and her mother had been in harmony instead of at odds. "Mother, we've gone through all this already. I'm not Sister Michael anymore."

A note of desperation entered her mother's voice. "That's like saying you're not tall anymore."

"I'm not," Claire pointed out calmly. She didn't have time for this.

"You know what I mean," Margaret insisted. "All right," she conceded, "bad example. It's like saying you're not Italian anymore." She nodded her head in triumph, as if feeling that she'd chosen her example well this time. "Saying it doesn't change things. You can't stop being Italian."

"Not the same thing, Mother, not the same thing at all." She saw tears suddenly gather in her mother's eyes. Guilt assaulted her at the same moment. She placed her arm around her mother's shoulders, or tried to. "Mother—"

But her mother shrugged her arm aside, moving away from her as if she had a contagious disease. "I'm going to die." Her tone was oddly resigned.

Her mother wasn't going to lick this thing if she'd already surrendered to it. She needed hope, Claire thought. A lot of it.

"No, you're not," she countered fiercely.

"Yes, I am. Because of you. You know this kind of thing doesn't go unpunished."

For one moment, Claire felt as if she'd been physically slapped across the face. Stunned, she focused on the larger subject. "You don't believe that."

"Yes, I do." There was no arguing with her mother's tone of voice.

If she couldn't talk her mother out of it, she could still elaborate on her own beliefs, Claire reasoned, hoping that, in time, it would make her mother come around. "Well, I don't. I don't believe in a petty God who insists on going tit for tat." She and God might not be on the same wavelength at the moment, but she still believed in His existence, still believed that He wasn't a vengeful God. Why would her mother even think that? It was her mother who had taught her everything she believed in.

Her mother turned away from her. When she spoke again, Claire thought her heart was going to break from just hearing the sorrow in her mother's voice. "Easy for you to say. You're not the one with acute leukemia."

All she could do was give her mother the benefit of her own faith. "Mother, I don't have a clue why some things happen, why some people have everything go right for them even if they don't seem to deserve it and why other people have so many bad things happen, even if they are good, decent people—"

"Maybe if you'd paid more attention at the convent, you'd have some of those answers."

She continued as if her mother hadn't interrupted. Her mother wasn't being fair, but she couldn't fault her. Staring at the face of your own possible mortality could frighten anyone. "But I do know that God doesn't sit around keeping score and threatening people with sores and pestilence if they get out of line."

A hopelessness descended over Margaret. "Then why am I sick?" she demanded.

Claire hugged her mother, trying desperately to comfort her. "I wish I knew, Mother. But I do know that you were diagnosed long before I ever left the order."

"He knew you were going to leave. He knows everything."

Rather than become annoyed or defensive, Claire felt nothing but compassion for what her mother was going through. But at the same time, she wanted her mother to be aware of how convoluted her thinking was.

"So what you're saying is that you're being punished for something I was *going* to do."

"Yes," Margaret declared with feeling, then relented. "No." She could feel an enormous headache building as the tension inside her increased. "Oh, I don't know." She pressed her lips together, looking at her only child. She did, in a selfish way, appreciate her being here but at the same time, she felt in her heart it was wrong. Claire belonged in the convent. And she had taken her away from that, no matter what Claire said to the contrary. "Everything was so much clearer a year ago," Margaret lamented.

Since she couldn't seem to help her mother, maybe someone else could. The woman had always been partial to priests. "Mother, I'm going to see if I can get Father Ryan to stop by later today."

Margaret's eyes widened in horror. "Oh, no, I couldn't face him."

Claire slipped into her black pumps. The moment

isolated itself. These were her first pair of non-sensible shoes in twenty-two years. She'd worn them the other night to Saturday's. She'd forgotten how much she enjoyed wearing high heels.

The next moment, she forced herself to concentrate on what her mother was saying. "Why?"

They were back on opposite ends of the discussion again. "You know why."

Walking out of her bedroom, Claire turned and took her mother's hands in hers. "Mother, you're going to have to get used to it. I've left the order, I'm not Sister Michael anymore. But I will always, *always* be your daughter. And I *am* going to take care of you, to be there for you whenever you need me—and even if you don't," she added with a smile. She dropped her hands and headed toward the stairs. "But right now, if I don't get going, I'm going to be late for my first day and you know what you've always said about first impressions—you never get a second chance to make one."

Following behind her on the stairs, Margaret sighed and shook her head. "Go," she ordered without any enthusiasm.

Reaching the bottom of the stairs, Claire waited for her mother to descend. Again she took her mother's hands in hers. When her mother didn't look at her, she tilted her head, moving into her mother's visual range. "Wish me luck?"

"Luck," Margaret murmured.

Well, it certainly didn't qualify as an enthusiastic pep-rally cheer, but it would have to do. "Good enough," Claire responded.

Releasing her mother's hands, she grabbed her purse and the small briefcase she'd packed and repacked twice last night. In it was the lesson plan she'd come up with as well as the curriculum the principal had given her after her interview had ended. At the time, he'd told her that there was no need for him to continue conducting his search for a replacement. As far as he was concerned, he'd found the person he was looking for.

Being hired on the spot did wonders for her self-esteem, which at that point was in danger of wavering, moving about like a flag in the wind.

Claire paused to kiss her mother's cheek. "Nancy's going to look in on you today," she informed her. "And be sure you have something to eat," she added.

Margaret looked listless, as if she'd lost the reason to live. "I'm not hungry."

"Not now, later."

"I won't be hungry later."

Nope, this wasn't going to be easy at all. How could she have forgotten how stubborn her mother could be? "Okay, I'll tell Nancy to force-feed you."

"So I can be struck down on a full stomach," Margaret murmured as she stood by the door.

"All the best people usually are," Claire agreed cheerfully, hoping to joke her mother out of the dour mood she'd descended into. "And tonight, when I come home, you and I are going to the movies." Whatever work she had to do to prepare for tomorrow, she could do after her mother fell asleep.

Her words garnered her a half smile from her mother.

Some way, somehow, Claire promised herself as she closed the front door and raced to the vintage vehicle in the driveway, she was going to find a way to make her mother accept her decision and come around.

* * *

Her first week went by far more smoothly than she'd anticipated. Though it had been a while since she'd taught, her last assignment taking full advantage of her nursing skills rather than her teaching abilities, the joy of working with young minds came flooding back.

Admittedly, the children she'd been assigned were quietly feeling her out. They didn't challenge her so much as they explored her boundaries, seeing if she was going to be very strict, the way Mrs. Butterfield had been, or a pushover, like their last substitute had turned out to be.

Claire was determined to fall somewhere in between the two.

Her experience, both with unruly students and with eager ones, had more than prepared her for her job. Right from the start, she made it clear that she was going to care about them, not as a class, but as individuals. She'd learned their names within the first half hour. She wanted to get to know each and every one of them, their likes, their dislikes, what they wanted to learn and what they had trouble learning.

In exchange for this information, she told them that it was only fair for them to get to know her. So just before recess on the first day, she threw open the floor and told them that they could ask her questions about herself.

Instantly, a sea of hands shot up. She pointed to the one farthest in the back. "Colin, go ahead."

The dark-haired boy grinned, obviously pleased that she'd remembered his name. "What did you do before you came here?"

Oh boy, the toughest one first, she thought. *Might as well get it out of the way.* She knew that she didn't have to be complete in her answer. She could say that she was a teacher and a nurse without bringing in the fact that she'd been part of a Catholic order while doing it. But inevitably, one of the children would find out and tell the others and keeping this from them would somehow make her seem dishonest.

"I was a Dominican Sister." The low level of noise, always present to some degree in a class that size and that age, disappeared as thirty-four sets of eyes looked at her in surprise. "I taught children in Africa. I also helped nurse them when they were sick. I have two degrees, one in nursing, one in teaching."

"Do you have a nun degree, too?" one of the children asked.

She smiled. "You need to raise your hand." The moment the words were out of her mouth, the hand shot up. "Debbie?"

"Do you have a nun degree, too?"

Explaining the differences to them between nuns and sisters might have been a wee bit too much for them right now, so she refrained from delving into the subject and simply accepted the term Debbie had used.

"You don't need to get a degree to be a nun," she told the girl. "You just join the order."

"But you don't want to join anymore? I mean—" Another little girl's hand shot up.

Amused, she nodded at the second girl who spoke out of turn. "Janice?"

"You don't want to be a nun anymore?"

Again, Claire went with the simplest answer. "My mother got sick and I wanted to be close by in case she needed me, so I left the order and found this wonder-ful job, teaching fourth-grade students. And here I am." She nodded at the boy on the side. "Billy?"

"Your mother still sick?"

"Yes, I'm afraid she is. But she's a little bit better now than she was and she has a lot of nice doctors taking care of her. She listens to what they tell her to do." Thank God for that, Claire added silently.

The bell rang just then, signaling her reprieve. "Okay, kids, recess. File out in an orderly manner. I'll see you back in forty-five minutes."

They didn't have to be told twice.

From that morning on, the children in Classroom 104 became *her* children and the groundwork for a warm rapport had been laid. By the time the principal looked in on her the afternoon of the second day, he seemed more than a little impressed with the way he found her conducting the class.

Despite the fact that he slipped out as quietly as he had come in, Claire was keenly aware of his visit. She noted with relief that he was nodding his head as he left.

Dropping by her classroom that Friday to officially ask her how her week had gone, Simon Walcott confided, "I had a good feeling about you when you came in, Ms. Santaniello. I'm glad I followed my in-stincts and hired you." He watched her pack up her briefcase. "Although I have to admit that I did have one reservation."

Claire stopped snapping the locks on her briefcase and looked up. "And that was?"

He crossed his arms before him. "That you might

find the students too difficult to handle and decide that you'd made a mistake by leaving the shelter of the Church."

She smiled and shook her head. "You might recall that on my resume, I mentioned that the Church sent me to Africa to teach and to treat the native population. That is *far* from being sheltered."

He looked a little embarrassed. "Yes, of course," he murmured stiffly. "I didn't mean any offense."

She began to think that it would take other people more time to figure out how to act around her now that she was no longer Sister Michael than it would for her to figure out how to act as a layperson.

"You didn't offend me, Mr. Walcott," she told him with a hint of amusement. "I just wanted to be sure that the record was straight."

"Consider it straightened," he told her with a smile. "And please, call me Simon." He walked her out of her classroom. "I want you to know that my door is always open if you have anything you need to discuss. Anything," he emphasized.

"I appreciate that. And now, if you'll excuse me, I have to get home to my mother." She'd told him when she'd interviewed for the job about her mother and the fact that sometime in the future, there might be days that she would need to take off, or even be forced to take a leave of absence. She'd done it to be completely up-front with him. To her relief, her honesty had served as a plus.

Like a man suddenly remembering a dance step that had eluded him, Walcott stepped out of her way. "Yes, of course, your mother. Tell her I hope she's doing well," he called after her.

"Thank you, I will."

And she would, too, Claire thought. She wanted her mother to know that there were a lot of people, even strangers, interested in her progress. It might make her mother feel not quite so alone.

The second week found Claire drawing yard duty during lunch. The secretary in charge of such assignments apologized, saying they were shorthanded and that it would have been Mrs. Butterfield's turn. Claire didn't mind. She liked watching the children in unstructured play. It gave her insight into who they really were.

She moved along the grounds, making sure that there were no temper tantrums thrown, no squabbles escalating into shoving matches. For the most part, everything went smoothly.

Just before recess was over, she was talking to several little girls who had approached her seemingly with a question but in reality just wanting to hang around her, culling her favor. As she played along, Claire's attention was drawn to a handful of fourth-grade boys—some of them from her class—standing around a short, slight boy with hair the color of midnight.

The other boys were taunting him. She could tell from the body language before she ever heard a word.

"Excuse me, girls." She separated herself from her new admirers and hurried over to the circle of boys. The object of their taunts had his back to her so she didn't get a good look at him until she was almost on top of the group.

As if sensing the presence of someone there to help, the boy turned his head toward her at the last moment.

For a second, Claire was caught completely off guard. Time didn't stand still, it receded from her, going backward. Back some twenty-six years. Although the boy who was being taunted had black hair, something about him made her remember Caleb. He had the same slight build, the same soulful, penetrating blue eyes, she realized.

Claire forced herself to focus. She looked from one boy's face to another. The moment she'd appeared, they'd fallen silent and were now studying the tips of their footwear.

"What's going on, boys?" she asked.

"Nothing, Miss Santaniello," Luke, one of the boys from her class, murmured, struggling to wrap his tongue around her last name.

"I'm glad to hear that," she said, slowly walking around the perimeter of the circle, looking at each boy one at a time. "I was afraid it might be 'something.' From where I was standing, it looked as if you boys were ganging up on—"

She paused for a moment, looking at the boy who, except for his hair color, could have been Caleb's doppelgänger if the past and the present could exist side by side. It was clear that she was waiting for him to fill in his name.

"Danny," he answered very quietly. "Danny McClain."

McClain. Same as Caleb. Caleb had said he had a son going to this school, but until a couple of minutes ago, she'd forgotten. It really was a small world, she thought.

"Hello, Danny McClain, I'm Miss Santaniello." She turned to the rest of the boys and continued, "It looked as if you boys were ganging up on Danny here. But I knew my boys wouldn't do something cowardly like that, would they?"

"No, Miss Santaniello," several of the other boys chorused, their voices awkwardly cutting into one another.

She nodded knowingly. "I didn't think so. You know, maybe you boys can help me out. I was just wondering how I was going to take all those big, heavy textbooks out of the supply closet. I could really use some big, strong guys to help." Her sweeping gaze included all five of the boys in her class, as well as Danny and the two others who'd made up the rest of the circle. "Think you could do that for me?"

Small chests puffed up and heads bobbed as a cacophony of assertive sounds rose in the affirmative.

She smiled broadly at them. "Terrific. Come this way." Claire began to lead the boys into the building, then realized that not all of them were following. Danny was hanging behind like a child accustomed to being excluded. "You, too, Danny."

The boy seemed surprised to be included, despite the fact that he had voiced a willingness to help. The other boys were all fourth-graders, while he belonged in third.

He blinked. "Me?"

"That's what I said." Putting an arm around his shoulders, she ushered him over toward the others, who looked a little annoyed at having this interloper thrust upon them. This, she promised herself, was going to change. "I want you boys to work together, all right?"

"Yes, Miss Santaniello."

The response, composed of mingling voices, was far from enthusiastic. But it was a start.

Chapter Five

She saw him through her window.

It was quite by accident. Working ahead, Claire was just trying to think of something exciting to add to her lesson plan for next week when she glanced up and saw him. Danny, walking by slowly in the schoolyard.

The small shoulders were slumped, as if he had the weight of the world on them. There'd been a sadness in his eyes earlier. She'd noticed it almost immediately when she'd looked at him during recess. The same sort of sadness she'd seen half a world away, in the eyes of the children living in a war-torn village where hope had been the first casualty.

It wasn't the way an eight-year-old was supposed to appear.

It took her less than a minute to make up her mind. The lesson plan could wait. Closing the large, black,

bound book, she quickly stuffed it into her worn briefcase. She snapped the locks shut as she rose from the
desk. Picking up the briefcase and her purse, she slung
the latter over her shoulder and sailed out of the room,
heading down the hallway. She set a new record getting
to the front door.

Hurrying down the steps, Claire turned right and was
just in time to intersect Danny's path out of the schoolyard.

Preoccupied, he walked right into her. The startled,
uneasy look faded instantly as he glanced up to see
who he'd bumped into.

"I'm sorry, Miss Santaniello," he apologized.

"No harm done." The boy was small for his age, just
like his father had been. "Looked like you were somewhere else far away," she commented. The thin shoulders beneath the blue-and-white striped T-shirt shrugged
in response.

Claire scanned the area. In the distance, parents
were parked, waiting for their children to find them so
they could take off. A few of the older students were
heading toward the bike racks where a small squadron
of bicycles were chained, waiting to be released.

She looked back at the boy before her. "Is anyone
picking you up from school?"

"No, ma'am." He shifted his sagging backpack,
raising it a little higher. "I walk home."

"I see." Something about the boy spoke to her.
Something that told her he needed someone to listen,
to open up to. "Would you like a ride?" she asked
impulsively.

That was when she realized that he'd been glancing
over toward a group of boys, some of whom were in

her class. He had to pass them in order to walk out the front gate.

Raising his eyes to hers, Danny seemed somewhat relieved.

"Yes, ma'am. Thank you." She smiled to herself. She didn't remember Caleb being this polite. Danny's mother had done a good job raising the boy. He fell into step with her as they headed toward the rear of the school and the parking lot. "My dad says I'm not supposed to get in a car with anybody but him or Mrs. Collins, but you're a teacher. You're okay." And then he looked just a tad hesitant as well as hopeful. "Right?"

"Well, your dad's right about not getting into a stranger's car." She couldn't stress this enough and had already talked to her class about it at the tail end of the first day. "But I'm more than okay," she assured him cheerfully. "And," she added as the deal maker, "I know your dad."

Her hand on his shoulder, she gently steered him toward the left side of the parking lot where she'd left her mother's car.

She was going to have to see about getting one of her own, she thought. At least a used one. She didn't like the idea of leaving her mother without transportation, even if Nancy had said she was more than willing to drive her mother anywhere she wanted to go. In addition, she and her mother did things like grocery shopping in the afternoon, after she got home from school. Still, she knew that the car was part of her mother's independence. She needed to look into getting a used car as soon as possible.

Danny was looking up at her in surprise. "You do? You know my dad?"

Reaching the Mustang, she unlocked the passenger-side door, then held it open for him. As Danny turned his back to her, she helped him off with his backpack. Again, he seemed surprised. She had a feeling that he was used to doing things on his own.

Claire dropped the backpack into the backseat. "Your dad's Caleb McClain, right?"

Danny climbed in and immediately reached for the seat belt to buckle up. Definitely well trained, she thought.

"Yes, that's my dad," Danny answered, nodding his head.

Rounding the hood, Claire got in on the driver's side. She grinned at the small boy. "Well, I used to babysit him."

There was no response from the passenger side. Danny stared at her for a long moment, his eyes opened so wide, he seemed in danger of having them fall out of his head. He sucked in his breath as she put her key in the ignition. Turning it, the cherry-red car rumbled and bucked to life.

"No way," Danny finally said, wonder pulsing from every letter.

"Way," Claire answered with a grin. She glanced behind her to make sure the path was clear. The lot was empty and she moved out.

"You don't look that old," Danny blurted out, still staring at her.

"Thank you for that." Glancing both ways, she pulled out onto the street, then turned her attention to something practical and pressing. "What's your address, Danny?" He rattled it off for her quickly. It turned out that he lived less than a mile away, in one of the developments that had been built during the time that she'd been gone from Bedford. "You're going to have to be my guide," she told him. They were on Jeffrey Road and she vaguely knew that the street was south of the development he lived in. "I'm not that familiar with that area."

"Okay," he answered, sitting up a little straighter. He obviously took his assignment seriously. "You go down this long block and then turn right by the Chicken Shack."

His voice sounded a little deeper as he continued to give her directions. If she didn't know better, she would have said he was a short adult. Glancing at him, Claire smiled to herself.

"You know, you look just like your dad did at your age."

The comparison stunned him. "My dad was my age?" he asked in wonder.

She knew how surprised she'd been the first time her mother had shown her a photograph of herself as a child with her own parents. It took her a while to wrap her mind around the fact that her mother hadn't always been this slender five-foot-two redhead. "He certainly was," she told the boy.

Danny leaned back in his seat, taking the information in. "Wow."

She liked all children, but even after knowing him only a few minutes, she could tell that Danny was something special.

"We all start out as little people and get bigger," she told him matter-of-factly. "Your dad was pretty much a handful back then. Getting into all sorts of stuff." In the beginning, he'd kept her on her toes, resenting the fact that a girl had been placed in charge of him. But eventually, budding hormones kicked in and he began to see her in a new light, she now realized. She spared Danny a quick look as she took another corner. "So, are you like that?"

"No, ma'am." He wiggled a little, as if his answer left him somewhat uncomfortable. She sensed a little mischief in the boy, which she'd always believed was a good thing, even if he didn't want to admit it.

"So, you live with your Dad." It wasn't really a question but a rhetorical statement since the boy had said he wasn't allowed in a car except with his father or the other person he'd named. She wondered why he hadn't mentioned his mother.

"Yes, ma'am."

"Who's Mrs. Collins?" Maybe his parents were divorced and that was the way he referred to Caleb's girlfriend.

"The old lady across the street who stays with me until my dad comes home."

Old. To someone Danny's age, that could be anyone twenty and up, she thought. "Where's your Mom?" she asked casually, glancing at his profile as she waited for him to answer.

She saw his face crumble. Her heart tightened in her chest in empathy even though she wasn't sure just what was coming.

Danny sighed deeply. "She's gone."

For a moment, there was silence. Claire tried to gauge what his answer meant. Had there been an acrimonious divorce? Had his mother just taken off with someone, leaving him behind?

Or…?

"Some bad guys killed her," the small voice said, barely rising to the level of a whisper. Danny turned his head and gazed out the side window. "Last year, when I was little," he added, talking to the glass.

"Oh, Danny, I'm so sorry." She ran her hand comfortingly along his arm, knowing just how he had to feel. That would explain the dark look on Caleb's face when she'd said what she had about him going home to his son and his wife, she realized suddenly. She turned back to watch the road. Why hadn't Caleb said anything? "You know, I lost my dad when I was just a little older than you," she told Danny.

Out of the corner of her eye, she saw the boy look at her in wonder.

"You did?" he cried.

"I did." Her father had succumbed to a heart attack at an incredibly young age. Thirty-nine wasn't nearly old enough to leave behind a wife and child, she'd always thought. "It's rough, isn't it?"

"Uh-huh." The situation built an instant camaraderie between them. Danny shifted in his seat. "My dad's real sad," he confided. "He doesn't want to play or anything anymore now that my mom's gone."

Claire tried to recall anything that looked or sounded half as lonely as Danny did at that very moment. She failed.

That evening, as he approached his house, it took Caleb a moment to place the vehicle parked beside his front curb. When he did recognize it, he assumed it had to be a coincidence. Someone else in town had to own a cherry-red vintage 1968 Mustang besides Claire Santaniello.

But one glance at the license plate told him that while there might be other cherry-red Mustangs out there on the road, this particular vehicle was Claire's.

He looked at the plate again, but he knew he hadn't made a mistake. He had a penchant for remembering details, he always had, a little trick that had not only helped him in school, but in being a detective.

Not that any of that mattered anymore. Nothing mattered anymore.

But, if he was being honest, he had to admit that on some far-off plane, his curiosity had been aroused.

What the hell was Claire doing here?

Had something happened to Danny? he suddenly wondered, a tightness seizing his chest. Wouldn't they have called him from the school if it had? He glanced down at the cell phone clipped to his belt, tilting it to see if there were any messages that had come in, their announcing beep muffled by the noise of everyday life around him.

There were no messages.

Which meant Danny was okay.

He let go of the breath he was holding. But then, why was Claire here?

Unlocking the front door, Caleb walked in and called out, "Mrs. Collins?" The woman always remained until he came home. But this time, he didn't hear the sound of shuffling feet as the moccasins she favored rubbed against the rug. She rarely lifted her feet high enough to break contact.

In response to his voice, Claire, a towel tucked around the front of her skirt like a makeshift apron, came walking out of his kitchen. For the moment, Danny was nowhere to be seen.

"Hi." She greeted him with a radiant smile. "She's not here. I told her I'd stay with Danny until you came home."

He stared at her. "What are you doing here?" he asked. His eyes narrowed as he looked at her expression. Would she be smiling if there was something wrong?

Caleb decided he really didn't know her all that well. A great deal of time had passed since they'd known one another at all.

He expected the worst because the worst usually happened. "Something happen to Danny?"

When she'd decided to stay, Claire had first called home to check on her mother, then called Nancy on her cell to make sure that everything was really all right because Nancy had promised to drop by her mother's during the day. Nancy had assured her that her mother was indeed doing well.

Her conscience temporarily at rest, Claire had turned her attention to the immediate problem at hand: Danny's all but decimated self-esteem.

"Yes," she answered cheerfully. "He's learned that he can cook."

Caleb could only stare at her as if she'd lost her mind. "What?"

"I'm having Danny help me prepare dinner."

"Dinner?" Caleb began to feel a definite kinship with a village idiot.

Claire's head bobbed in response. Wisps of soft red hair that had come undone from the pins she'd placed to keep it up moved independently, making her look like some kind of storybook fairy with an apron. "Uh-huh. As I recall you used to love to eat."

"I don't love anything anymore." The words had just come out of their own accord, but ultimately, it was the truth. His capacity to love died the same moment that Jane had drawn her last breath.

"Except Danny," Claire corrected, her eyes warning him that there was only one acceptable answer to what was phrased as a coaxing question.

"Yeah—" he shoved his hands into his pockets "—except Danny. That goes without saying."

And he did, Caleb thought defensively. He *did* love his son, but he couldn't seem to display it. He felt trapped, separated from everything around him by a wall of thick glass. He could see everything, but touch nothing, reach nothing. It was all just out there, just beyond him.

So the best that he could do was provide for his son and see that the boy was taken care of. If the boy wasn't getting his quota of demonstrative love, he'd make it up to Danny down the line. Soon. Just not now. Not yet.

"But it should be said," Claire told him gently. "And often."

Not wanting to get into an argument, he ignored what she said. "Where is he?" Caleb asked, looking around the room.

"In the kitchen. C'mon."

She led the way back as if this wasn't his house and he didn't know his way around. Did she always take over like this? He tried to remember, but his childhood memories were clouded with prepubescent budding surges of lust and desire.

"We didn't have all that much to work with," she confessed, even though, midway through, she'd made a quick run to the grocery store with Danny. "But we did the best we could." She turned toward her energetic assistant. "Didn't we, Danny?"

Danny, wearing a makeshift towel/apron jauntily about his middle just like Claire, was kneeling on a stool that in turn was butted up against the counter. There were splotches of flour on his face and hands, not to mention on different sections of his torso, the "apron" not withstanding.

The boy's eyes, Caleb thought, looked brighter than he'd seen for a long while. Something very distant within him was glad.

"What is all this?" he asked in a voice that comprised equal parts of bridled impatience and confusion.

"Dinner. It's called chicken la—" Stumped, Danny looked over toward his mentor for help.

"Chicken à la King," Claire supplied brightly. "I told Danny that was your favorite."

If the woman smiled any wider, her lips were going to split, Caleb thought, annoyed. He didn't want anybody in his house when he came home at the end of the day. He just wanted to retreat in peace. Having Claire here forced him to at least be semisociable.

"Yeah, a long time ago." He shook his head as if to clear it. Dinners ordinarily were delivered by adolescents with either a pizza embossed on the side of their car, or a fading green dragon with a bobbing head affixed on the top of their roof. To his knowledge, there was next to nothing except for beer, milk and bread in his refrigerator. "Where did the chicken come from?"

"The grocery store," she answered without missing a beat. "I did a little shopping," she confessed and glanced at the boy on the stool. "Danny helped."

"What is it that you're doing here—besides cooking?" he said before she could restate the obvious.

"I drove Danny home."

Caleb glanced over at his son, who seemed to be intent on the job he'd been assigned. "Danny walks home."

"I know, he told me," she said, absolving the boy of any wrongdoing in case Caleb thought that Danny had asked her to bring him home. "But this time, I thought he needed a ride."

Caleb looked over to see if there was any telltale sign of injury somewhere on his son's person. There wasn't. If he wasn't hurt, why couldn't he just walk home the way he always did?

"Why?"

This looked as if it was going to get complicated, Claire thought. She made an impulsive decision.

"Excuse us for a second, Danny. Keep stirring," she instructed. Danny nodded solemnly and did as he was told. Claire hooked her arm through Caleb's and led the surprised-looking man off to the side, where, unless he suddenly started shouting, their voices wouldn't carry. "Did you know that he gets picked on at school?"

No, he hadn't known, Caleb thought, keeping his face immobile. Danny had never said anything. He grew defensive of his son.

"He can take care of himself."

"Can he?" she pressed. Before he could answer, she continued, trying to make him aware of what he should have already known. "He's not you, Caleb. He's a much sadder, withdrawn little boy. And that makes him a perfect victim for bullies. I defused one situation today and I'll look out for him on the school grounds as much as I can, but while I was driving him home, he talked a little—" Caleb looked at her sharply. "Just enough for me to find out that you lost your wife."

Indignation rose within him. He felt as if he'd been invaded. "That's not any business of yours, Claire."

"We're all connected in this world and you're my friend. And you and your son are both hurting," she pointed out, making her case. "I think that makes it my business."

"Danny's okay," he insisted.

But Claire shook her head. When he turned away, she grabbed his arm, pulling him back around. Forcing him to listen. "Danny lost his mother—and, from what I'm picking up, just possibly his father, as well. That definitely is not okay."

Because this was Claire, he struggled to hang on to a temper that had become dangerously frayed this last year. "Look, I appreciate what you're trying to do—"

"Do you? From where I'm standing it looks to me as if you think I'm butting in."

His eyes narrowed. But try as he might, a section of him couldn't fault her. "Well, aren't you?"

"Yes," she said without reservation, completely taking the wind out of his sails.

"Miss Santaniello, it's bubbling," Danny called out to her urgently.

The discussion they were having would wait. "Excuse me, my assistant needs help."

She left Caleb speechless and staring.

Chapter Six

"You're not going to stay?" Danny asked, watching her pick up her purse.

The dinner was made and she and Danny had finished setting the table. He'd looked a little confused when she'd had him put out only two place settings but he didn't voice his concern until after she'd brought out the food and he saw her getting ready to leave.

Caleb had said nothing, moving off to the side and observing the activity in silence. She was aware that at one point, he'd been watching her every move and she couldn't gauge if he was holding his tongue out of politeness or if some other emotion governed him. Heaven knew his expression wasn't readable. He probably made a marvelous poker player.

Pushing her purse strap up on her shoulder, Claire paused to lightly run her hand through the boy's thick dark hair. With affection, she brushed some away from his eyes. His hair was a little long, a little shaggy, but she liked that. If he followed his father's path, she judged that Danny would be an undoubted heart-breaker in another few years. Caleb, she had to con-cede, was an extremely handsome man.

"I think your dad would prefer that it's just the two of you for dinner," she told him.

She glanced over toward the family room a few feet away. Caleb sat on the sofa, flipping through channels at an exceptionally fast clip and pretending not to listen—but she could tell by the tilt of his head that he was.

Danny turned his head to look at his father, clearly disappointed by the turn of events. "Can't you tell him you're staying, Miss Santaniello?" Danny asked. "You're a teacher. He can't say no."

It was painfully obvious that the boy was hungry for attention and affection, Claire thought. This was some-thing that needed to be worked out and she fully intended to do it. More than anything, she felt that that sort of thing was her mission, her calling. But for the time being, she'd butted in as far into this family as she could.

"It doesn't work that way, Danny," she told him. "This is your dad's house and I can't just invite myself to dinner."

"Why not?" Caleb asked, rising and crossing over to her and his son. The question took Claire entirely by surprise. "You invited yourself in to cook."

"Well, you and Danny needed to have something for dinner," she explained, then spread her hands inno-cently. "Inviting myself to share that dinner might be taking too much for granted."

Caleb's expression remained somber. He circled her slowly. A tiny, distant part of him delighted in putting his babysitter on the spot. Just how much surprised him. The ache created by watching her go through the same paces in the kitchen that Jane used to also surprised him. He forced himself to squelch a bittersweetness wrapped in anger.

"And what you did up until now isn't?" he asked.

Claire never wavered. She'd faced down hostile soldiers bent on wiping out the village where she was ministering. Caleb McClain was a pussycat in comparison. She raised her eyes to his. "You would have told me to leave if it was."

Fair enough, he thought. "I'm not telling you to leave now."

Her lips widened in a smile. "Is that a backward invitation?"

Glancing at Danny, she saw that his more somber mood was dissolving, replaced by a glimmer of hope.

Something exceedingly maternal stirred within her. He was a darling, darling boy. If she'd had children, she would have wanted a son just like Danny.

"You cooked it, you might as well stay to have some," Caleb said, shrugging. Moving past her, he raised the lid from the Dutch oven on top of the burner. "Looks like you made enough to feed an army."

Claire slid her purse strap off her arm, leaving her purse on the counter. "No, just a couple of hungry men." She ruffled Danny's hair and he grinned at her. "As I recall," she said to Caleb, "you liked leftovers."

For a long moment, Caleb said nothing, he just watched her. When he'd first realized who she was at the restaurant the night he came to her rescue, a fragment of pleasure had surfaced. Just for a second. But in the face of the tragedy that existed in his past, pleasure didn't last and so that fragment quickly faded.

Both then and now, he wanted nothing to disturb the equilibrium he'd managed to reach. It allowed him to function, which was the only thing he was concerned about. If he couldn't feel, so much the better. It kept the pain from destroying him. In the long run, though he might not agree now, it was also best for Danny. At least his son wouldn't see him have a meltdown.

But having Claire here put an immense strain on the locks of the gate that kept out all that pain, all those feelings.

"You recall too much," he told her, his voice as flat as the Mojave Desert.

"Maybe you don't recall enough," Claire countered. Her voice was light, but the look in her eyes burrowed right through him. It made him momentarily regret his offhanded invitation. But before he could say anything, the woman who had made herself so at home in his house turned toward his son. "Let's go wash up, Danny."

Rather than protest that he hadn't gotten dirty, Danny happily fell into step beside her, leaving him standing there, watching the two of them walk off. Just as he'd once walked off with Jane.

Caleb tried to remember the last time he'd seen his son smile like that and couldn't.

It suddenly dawned on him that Claire knew where the downstairs bathroom was. That made her entirely too familiar with his house. While she had been the "woman of his dreams" for probably half a dozen years, now that he was no longer a wide-eyed, innocent adolescent, he didn't want this woman—or anyone else—barging into his house and his life.

So why the hell did you let her stay?

There was no doubt in Caleb's mind that she had somehow orchestrated the situation in order to coax the words out of his mouth. And she had snapped the invitation up like a hungry baby bird at mealtime.

So she'd eat and go, he reasoned, walking to the table. What harm could it do?

He learned the hard way.

Claire didn't just eat and go. She ate and talked. And talked. And talked. Fashioning conversations that pulled him in, that forced him to contribute. He tried to keep his responses to monosyllabic yeses and nos, but he was badly out-gunned.

As for his son, well for once, Danny sounded closer to the way he'd been before Jane died, something he hadn't been for the last year.

Caleb knew that was a good thing. He didn't want Danny to suffer, didn't want the boy to endure the kind of pain that he did. And if he couldn't reach out to the boy, Caleb was grateful that at least Claire could.

The Chicken à la King was almost gone, as was the flavored rice she'd made to accompany the main course. She tilted the serving spoon, ready to press it back into use.

"Thirds?" she asked, looking from father to son and then back again.

Danny shook his head, his small hands pressed against his aching abdomen. "Uh-uh, I'm going to explode."

She grinned. He'd eaten well, she thought with a

feeling of triumph. The boy was decidedly too thin. "Can't have that." Her eyes shifted over toward Caleb. "What about you? Want another helping or are you going to explode, too?"

Several cryptic responses materialized in his mind, but he let them go. She'd worked far too hard to deserve a sarcastic remark, so he merely shook his head in reply. "No."

The single word didn't exactly answer her question in full. This was like pulling teeth. She missed the boy she remembered, the one who used to like to talk to her.

"Does that mean no you're not going to explode and that you want more?"

"If I'd wanted more," he informed her evenly, "I would have taken more."

She looked at his empty plate. He'd had two servings. Had that been prompted by some reserved politeness? He'd made no comment about the dinner. She drew her own conclusion.

"Then you didn't like it?"

Caleb's scowl deepened. "I didn't say that."

"No," she agreed, speaking as slowly, as deliberately as he did. She found it quickly tired out her jaw. He was too rigid, she thought, but knew there was no way she could get him to relax. "You didn't."

Her expression was a mixture of wistfulness and disappointment, Caleb realized. Watching those emotions pass over her face did something strange and unsettling to his insides. He didn't like it.

"You didn't say much of anything," Claire went on to note.

He could have sworn she was about to add something to that, but then, the next moment, she had turned her attention toward his son, relieving him of the obligation of having to make some sort of response.

"Would you like to help me wash the dishes?" she asked Danny as she brought the last of the dishes to the kitchen and placed them on the counter next to the sink.

Danny eyed her, a bit confused. "We've got a dishwasher for that." He pointed to the stainless-steel appliance that was comfortably seated between the oven and the cabinets below the sink.

"So do I," Claire told him. "Two of them." To illustrate her point, she held up her hands. Looking at Danny, she nodded at his hands and added pointedly, "So do you."

The small, innocent face scrunched. "No, we have a machine." This time, he opened the dishwasher door, showing her the racks meant to hold the various plates, glasses and utensils.

Very gently, Claire moved aside his hand and closed the door again. "That uses up electricity." She seated the rubber stopper over the drain, pushing it down to secure the seal. "Besides, I like doing dishes."

This was obviously something Danny had never considered before. "You do?"

"Yup." Claire began shifting the dishes into the sink. "Washing dishes gives people a chance just to stand around and talk while they're getting something accomplished." She glanced over her shoulder at Caleb. He was standing off to the side, his arms folded before him as he took the scene in silently. As before, the expression on his face locked her out. She hadn't a clue what he was thinking. "You're welcome to come join us," she told him cheerfully.

Danny raised his eyes to his father's face. He didn't

say a word, but it was clear that he was waiting for an answer. A positive one.

"No" hovered on Caleb's lips, but a trace of amusement, its roots in a long-ago yesterday, forced it back. He straightened and left the shelter of the doorway. "You're still bossy, aren't you?"

Claire examined his question for a moment, giving it honest consideration. She was the soul of innocence when she answered, "I never thought of myself as being bossy. I just take charge."

Caleb laughed shortly, shaking his head. He walked back into the dining room, then returned bearing the all-but-depleted serving dish. He placed it on the counter, leaving it up to her to dispose of.

"Same thing."

Her amusement never wavered. Danny's eyes darted back and forth between the two of them.

"No, it's not," she told Caleb. Taking a smaller bowl out of the cupboard, she transferred what was left of the Chicken à la King into it, then deposited the serving bowl into the sink. "Being bossy is ordering people around for some sort of self-gratification. I just try to get things done in the most efficient way."

"And you consider washing dishes by hand to be the most efficient?" Caleb asked.

He watched as Danny brought two fistfuls of utensils from the dining room and placed them on the side of the sink. She'd trained the boy with hardly a word, he noted. But then, she'd pretty much done that with him when he was around Danny's age.

"I do," Claire said. Swinging the faucet over to the adjoining sink, she turned up the water, testing it. It became hot almost instantly.

She smiled at him, that killer smile that he'd always thought eclipsed everything else. It hadn't changed, hadn't faded. He still found himself being pulled in. Just as he had years back. Except that this time around, he recognized it for what it was. Sheer attraction.

And that worried him.

"You know I'm right," Claire said.

She noticed Caleb's dumbfounded expression. It was probably going to take him a while before he realized that this little exercise with plates and sudsy water was getting him to interact with his son. But eventually it would dawn on him. Hopefully by then, Caleb would be at least partially on his way to recovery.

Turning her mind to the job at hand, Claire opened the cabinet just beneath. She smiled to herself. In some ways, Caleb was a creature of habit. His mother used to keep the garbage container directly beneath the sink and so did he. She scraped off the plates—although she noted with a sense of pride that there wasn't all that much to scrape—and then placed the plates into the sink. Finished, she took the utensils that Danny held out to her and then the glasses. The latter, Caleb had gathered.

Progress.

"Where do you keep your dishwashing detergent?" Even as she asked, she crouched down and looked at the various items stored to the left of the garbage container.

"I don't," Caleb informed her flatly. He pointed to a bright green bottle butted up against a spray container of carpet cleaner. "There's a bottle of detergent for the dishwasher. It's all I've got."

Undaunted, she nodded. "Good enough. It's basically the same thing," she told Danny. He was watching her every move. Impulsively, she gave him a quick, one-arm hug before continuing. He looked surprised, and then pleased.

Which melted her heart.

Taking the detergent out, she turned on the hot water, then poured a capful of detergent just beneath the running stream. Instantly, suds began to form, multiplying at a prodigious rate and spreading out to claim the entire surface within the sink.

She glanced at Danny, who watched the display intently. She caught the inside of her lip to keep from laughing. "It's like a bubble bath for dishes," she told the boy.

He nodded, mesmerized by the mounting suds that were growing higher and higher by the moment. "Cool."

This time she did laugh. "You took the words right out of my mouth, Danny." And then she reached for the sponge. "Okay, assignments." She looked at the boy. "I'll wash, you dry."

Danny picked up the closest dish towel and moved back next to her. He slanted a glance toward his father. "Is Dad going to do anything?"

"Supervise," Caleb answered. There was finality in his tone.

But Claire had never let a little thing like that stop her. "Supervise is good," she agreed. And then she eyed Caleb, giving him the benefit of her penetrating green eyes. He would have to have been blind to miss the humor in them. "Putting the dishes away is even better."

He shrugged, leaning against the counter. "Like I said, bossy."

Carefully avoiding his father's eyes, Danny beckoned to her, taking a step back. Inclining her head, she bent down to his level.

"Is he supposed to say that to a teacher?" Danny asked in a hushed whisper, worried that his father had crossed some line. He liked her and didn't want anything to drive her away. He hadn't felt this good inside for a very long time and he was bright enough to know that it was because of her.

"I'm not sure," she told Danny, trying her best to sound as if she was taking his question seriously. "But your dad is also my friend from a long time ago, remember? That makes it okay. Friends sometimes talk funny to friends."

Danny seemed relieved. His grin crinkled up to his eyes and lit up the room. "Oh, yeah, I forgot."

Caleb looked from his son to the woman who had somehow invaded his home with next to no effort at all. He couldn't remember the last time Danny had appeared so relaxed. So like a little boy. He was grateful for that.

"Forgot what?" Caleb asked Danny.

"Miss Santaniello said she babysat you when you were my age." Danny gazed at him solemnly, as if unable to wrap his mind around the concept. "Were you *really* my age, Dad?"

Rather than address his son, Caleb looked at her instead. There was something unfathomable in his eyes, something that placed a barrier between them. She felt for him, felt the pain that had caused him to erect these invisible bars that kept everyone, including his son, at

bay. At the same time, she promised herself to disman-
tle them.

"Not that I recall," he answered.

He meant that, she thought. He was only thirty-
four, but his childhood was aeons away, kept at bay
because of the tragedy he'd endured. The tragedy that
could eventually be the end of him.

Claire turned toward Danny, deliberately keeping
her voice cheerful. She could only imagine what the
boy had experienced by proxy, having a father who
was so emotionally closed off. "He was, and he looked
exactly like you," she told the boy. "Except for the
hair," she qualified affectionately.

In response, Danny stood a little straighter and dried
the dish that he was holding. It was clear, to anyone
who bothered to notice, that Danny worshipped his
father.

Claire couldn't help wondering if Caleb was aware
of that. Probably not.

Chapter Seven

"**I**'m sorry I made you uncomfortable earlier, talking about your wife."

Claire and Caleb stood outside his house. She'd intended on remaining only until the dishes were done and put away, but then Danny wanted to show her a science project that was giving him trouble. So, after calling home and talking to her mother, who, she was happy to find out, was entertaining a couple of friends who'd dropped by, Claire had stayed to give Danny a little help mingled with encouragement. Before she knew it, the evening had melted away. Yawning, Danny reluctantly bid her goodnight and went to bed. Startled at how quickly the time had flown, Claire commented that she needed to be going herself.

Caleb gave her no argument, which didn't surprise

her. He did offer to walk her to her car, even though it was only parked a few feet away.

Since they were alone, Claire decided that now might be the time to apologize. She didn't want Caleb to think that she'd purposely barged in.

When she finished, Caleb nodded, as if to say that it was all right. What he left unsaid was that this was a sensitive subject for him, but no words were necessary. She could tell his sincerity by his expression. Questions rose in her head, questions she knew she couldn't ask. Not yet, anyway.

And then Caleb opened the door a crack. "Exactly what did Danny say when he told you about…losing his mother?"

Claire paused for a moment to recall the exact words Danny had used. "That some 'bad guys' killed her."

They stood on the wraparound porch, the single feature that had sold him on the house. He'd envisioned himself with Jane, facing their declining years, sitting here and rocking, enjoying each other's company. He hadn't sat on the porch in a year.

Caleb looked away, his face growing dark, foreboding. All trace of the boy she'd once known had completely vanished. "Yeah, that pretty much describes it."

His tone told her to keep away and she knew she should, but she was who she was and she couldn't just ignore the pain she knew was there. "Caleb, I'm so very sorry—"

His face hardened. How many times had he heard that phrase? How many times had he been forced to say it himself to the family of a victim?

"'For my loss,'" he supplied coldly. "Right." He turned to see the surprise in her eyes. "That *was* what you were going to say, wasn't it?"

The words sounded so very trite, even if they were heartfelt. The depth of real sentiment was hard to convey, even between friends. "No, that wasn't what I was going to say."

"Then what?" he challenged, unable to curb his bitterness.

"I was going to say that I'm really, really sorry that you're hurting, Caleb. You have no idea how sorry I am. But I think that you're letting the depth of your own pain blind you to the fact that Danny's hurting, too."

Of course his son was hurting. He knew that. But Danny hadn't lost the reason for his very existence, for taking a breath, the way he had. Caleb shrugged. "He's a kid."

"Kids have feelings, too," she said gently. "Heartbreak has no age or height requirement." She could tell that she was annoying him, but she couldn't make herself back off. Instincts told her there was too much at stake. Danny needed him. And, whether he knew it or not, he needed Danny in order to get through this. "Have you comforted him?"

Caleb looked at her as if she was talking nonsense. "What, held him and said it was going to be 'all better' soon? Danny's a smart kid, Claire. He knows it won't be."

She ignored the sarcasm. "No, I mean have you talked to him about his mother, about how much she loved him and that she's looking down on him now?"

Caleb laughed shortly and she found herself

thinking that she'd never heard anything so heart-wrenchingly sad. "You still believe that?"

Just because she'd shed her habit, just because she harbored doubts on one level, didn't mean that she had surrendered her faith. It was just under temporary reconstruction, that was all. She still believed, still prayed, still felt that there was a God who watched over them.

"Yes, I do," she answered without hesitation. "It's what gets me through the day. And the night."

Caleb shook his head. "What gets me through mine is not thinking." His eyes met hers. "About *any* of it."

"You don't have that luxury," she informed him, passion entering her voice. "You're not alone." She waved her hand toward the house. "That little boy worships you and he needs to know his dad is there for him."

Where did she get off, coming into his life after a twenty-two-year hiatus and just presuming that she had the right to tell him how to live his life? He felt his temper flaring and struggled to tamp it down. He didn't want to yell at her, but it wasn't easy refraining.

"Of course I'm there for him. I put a roof over his head and order takeout to feed him when bossy ex-nuns don't commandeer my kitchen."

She wasn't sure if he was trying to push her away or if that was a last-minute attempt at humor. Either way, she decided that maybe this was a good time to put him on notice.

"You're going to have to do a lot better than that if you want to get rid of me, Caleb," she informed him. "Just so you know, I don't push away that easily."

Caleb shoved his hands into the back pockets of his

jeans, glancing up at a sky that was still relatively light. He liked the dark better. It suited his mood.

Using more diplomacy than usual, he tried to choose his words carefully. "Look, I appreciate what you think you're trying to do, but I've got to deal with Jane's death in my own way."

"Is it working?" she challenged.

She'd lost him. All he wanted was for her to stop poking at this wound he carried around with him and go home. There was a bottle of whiskey in the house waiting to renew his acquaintance. Alcohol was the only thing that dulled the pain.

"What?" he finally bit off.

"'Your own way,'" she clarified. "Is it working?" Before he could say anything, she answered the question for him. "I don't think so." Her eyes held his for a long moment. "You haven't moved on."

"Maybe I don't want to move on," Caleb grounded out through lips that were barely moving.

He turned from her and she found herself addressing his back. "Again, you don't have that luxury. You're not going to forget her if you stop spending a chunk of each day silently railing at God for His injustice. Some of that pain that's eating you up inside is always going to be there, but it can be managed if you try. I'm guessing that Jane wasn't the kind of woman who would have wanted you to let your pain fester and suck out your soul."

It didn't matter what Jane would have wanted. This was how things were. Caleb blew out a ragged breath. "Sometimes, you have no choice."

Claire put her hand on his arm, silently letting him know that he wasn't alone. That she was there for him whenever he needed to talk. Whether he wanted her to be or not.

"You *always* have a choice, Caleb. And you're lucky enough not to be alone." He turned to her. "You have a wonderful boy in there and he needs you very, very much. Be there for Danny. *Really* be there for him." A fond expression slipped over her lips as she let her mind drift back across the years. "The Caleb that I remember was a joyful boy. Most likely," she guessed, "that was probably what attracted Jane to you in the first place."

He leaned against the railing, crossing his arms before him as he gazed out into the slowly descending twilight. "You know, it's really ironic. Here I am, a vice detective. Danger's built into the job. Every day, I run the risk of not coming home." He felt his throat threatening to close up on him. "And *she's* the one who got shot. *She's* the one who was killed."

"How did it happen?" Claire gently prodded.

First there was silence. It stretched out so far that she thought he was ignoring her question. Just when she was about to give it one more try, she heard his voice.

When he spoke, it was to the growing darkness, not to her. "She was a social worker. And fearless, utterly fearless. She insisted on working the worst cases, going into neighborhoods that cops didn't even want to go into without backup. When I asked her not to, she said—" his mouth twisted cynically "—she said her guardian angel would look out for her."

He blew out a breath, bracing himself for the rest of it. He felt Claire's hand on his arm again, and in some strange, odd way, it gave him strength.

"Well, her guardian angel must've been taking a lunch break that afternoon. Jane got caught in cross fire. Two rival gangs trying to lower their numbers. Instead, they killed her. They didn't even know it until the homicide detectives caught up to them." His voice shook with rage he didn't even bother trying to suppress. "She was that insignificant to them, to those bastards she was trying to help."

"She wasn't insignificant," Claire insisted with feeling. "Jane was making a difference."

That was such a load of crap, he thought angrily. He glared at Claire accusingly. "She could have made a difference somewhere else. She could've just stayed home and made a difference here—" he hit his chest with his fist "—in my life. In Danny's."

Claire realized that there were tears in Caleb's eyes, tears that instantly ripped her heart out. Compassion welled up within her, spilling out all over. Knowing no other way to comfort a soul in anguish, Claire did what came naturally to her. She put her arms around him.

At first, Caleb resisted, trying to pull back. Claire continued holding on to him, blocking his resistance. She surprised him with her strength.

And then something just broke inside him, shattering into a million pieces. He felt everything crumble within him.

He hadn't talked about Jane's death, not with anyone. Not with his partner, Ski, or even with Jane's father when he had to call the man to tell him that Jane had been killed. He had just given her father the bare details, remaining stoic, struggling to keep from falling apart himself.

Jane's father had blamed him for her death, saying

it'd been up to him as her husband to talk her out of taking those kinds of risks.

Her father's accusation just made him feel that much guiltier.

Though he'd tried to shrug her off at first, Claire refused to be pushed away. Refused to let him turn away. She just held him tighter. And then she felt him heaving with sobs that he had refused to set free.

Standing there, on her toes, she continued to hold him, stroking his hair and murmuring words of comfort just as if he were still the boy that she had taken care of so many years ago.

With all her heart, she wished there was something more positive she could do for him.

Even as she made the wish, she knew it wasn't possible. She held fast to the positive note that she'd gotten Caleb to open up, something she was fairly confident that he hadn't done up until now. Maybe it was the first step toward healing.

At least she could hope.

When she thought about it later—and she did, at great length—Claire really had no idea just how it actually came about.

No idea how an embrace meant to convey compassion and sympathy turned into something else. One moment, she was empathizing with the pain she knew Caleb had to be feeling, the sense of loss; the next moment, the close proximity between them created a feeling that went beyond compassion. It heated her from the inside out as well as from the outside in.

She'd been so removed from the secular world, so uninvolved in the intense kind of feelings that could erupt between a man and a woman, that she honestly didn't realize what was going on until it had already taken her to another level. Her romantic experiences before she'd joined the order had been grounded in youthful fantasies and imaginings.

She'd never even been kissed.

Until now.

She didn't even know how his lips had found hers.

Until they did.

Anything she might have imagined as a young girl didn't even begin to scratch the surface.

The closest she could compare it to was one of those amusement park rides that turned you upside down and shook you every which way before returning you to your original spot.

She felt disoriented and yet there was this wild rush inside her. And electricity. A great deal of electricity, crackling and humming between them. It took everything she had not to just fall into the kiss and remain there.

But she couldn't. It wasn't right. Gathering her strength to her, she forced herself to pull back.

Her breath felt trapped in her throat. And she was dizzy. She, who had never once been lost for words, now felt as if she'd suddenly been struck dumb.

It took him more than a moment to pull himself together. Even so, when Caleb lifted his head, he looked at the woman before him in stunned wonder. A second ago, she'd been hugging him and something had just given way inside him. He was the last word in stoicism and control, yet this one time he had allowed a sob of raw anguish to tear free and make its way up his throat.

The pain he had been harboring had been so high, so wide that he hadn't realized until just this moment that something else was going on at the same time. Something as basic as pain but a great deal more stirring. And, in its final analysis, a great deal more pleasurable, as well.

The physical attraction he'd suddenly become aware of had blindsided him. Twenty-two years ago he'd had a crush on the girl, but this was the woman before him and it wasn't a crush, wasn't some fleeting infatuation. He was leagues beyond feelings so shallow. What he had just felt, what he was still *feeling,* was far more powerful. Too powerful for a man as ultimately vulnerable as he was to resist. It was almost as if it had a mind of its own.

Before he could stop to analyze what he was doing, before he could stop himself from acting, Caleb had turned and brought his mouth down to hers.

And kissed her.

The second their lips touched, it was as if some kind of explosion had gone off inside him. His emotions were no longer all bound up, no longer mummified. They were ripping free of their shackles. He couldn't begin to describe or explain exactly what was going on, only that something very basic, something very sweet, was sweeping him away to an opened space with no walls, no ceilings, no barriers of any kind.

There was no way to define it except for the sensations bounding through him.

Caleb cupped the back of her head, as if he needed to anchor himself in place. While it lasted, he wanted to absorb the electrical impulses shooting off, right and left, jolting his system to a state of alert wakefulness that had been denied him this past year.

Startled, afraid of the intensity she was feeling, it was Claire who ultimately separated them from each other.

Once Caleb's lips left hers, she realized that she'd been very close to suffocating. The air she was drawing into her lungs arrived there in something just short of deep gulps. Her pulse was beating so frantically it took her more than a full moment to get her bearings. She became aware that Caleb was saying something to her.

The words felt as if they were just floating by her head. What had just happened here? Was this normal? It felt too good not to be bad, and yet, how could something so wondrous *be* bad?

She had to concentrate hard in order to make sense out of what he was telling her.

He seemed upset. No, concerned, she amended. She took in another deep breath. The fog around her brain began to lift.

"I'm sorry," Caleb was saying. "I didn't mean to upset you."

Upset? Was that what she was feeling?

No, she didn't think so. Disoriented, confused, dazed maybe, but not upset. Taking care not to hyperventilate, she slowly took another deep breath, willing her pulse to slow down to the speed of sound rather than light. Satisfied that she was decelerating to that level, Claire looked at him. The word *wow* started to pulse and throb through her brain like an over-lit neon sign.

"Did I look upset?" she asked him.

Caleb appraised her for a long moment, silently upbraiding himself for getting so carried away—although he *had* enjoyed it. A great deal. Which made it all the worse.

"No," he finally said, the oppressive guilt he'd momentarily experienced mercifully receding. "You look how I feel."

"And that is?" she prodded.

"Confused."

She nodded. That would be one word for it, she thought. Another would be *bewildered*. More words floated through her brain. Words like *bewitched, bedazzled*. Belatedly, she became aware that she was drifting into an old song from the fifties.

But that was just it, she realized. He'd made her whole being sing.

Claire inclined her head in an affirmative motion. "I'll accept that."

Caleb continued to look at her. He wanted to pull her into his arms and kiss her again. And again. And not stop until—

He dragged his hand through his hair, looking away. What the hell was happening here? "Oh God, Claire, nothing makes sense anymore."

She said to him what she would have said to anyone. What she'd told herself when qualms of insecurity assaulted her. "Give it time, Caleb. Just give it time and it will."

To her surprise, he turned to look at her, a challenge in his blue eyes. "How much time?" he asked. It seemed to him that the confusion, the pain, was only getting worse, not better.

The laugh that left her lips was dry and so not typical of her. "If I knew that, Caleb, I could probably make a great deal of money."

The tension slipped away. His mouth curved as he shook his head. "No, not you. You'd probably give it all to charity."

He sounded as if he had her right up there with Mother Teresa. There was a world of difference between them, Claire thought. She smiled, shaking her head. "I'm not exactly a saint, Caleb."

Without meaning to, he pressed his lips together before responding. The unique, sweet taste that was her came to him. Making him smile.

Granted, it was a small offering, but very reminiscent of the boy who, Claire firmly believed, still lived somewhere within the man.

"No," Caleb allowed, "I guess maybe you're not quite a saint."

She struggled not to blush. No way was she going to comment on what he'd just said. Instead, she turned to the matter of his well-being. "Are you feeling a tiny bit better?" she asked him.

"I don't know about 'better.' Shell-shocked might be more appropriate." And then he grew serious again. "I didn't mean to offend you."

"You didn't."

He watched her for a long moment. Their relationship had never been anything but honest. One of the reasons he'd liked her so much was because she never talked down to him, never treated him as if he were a child to her "adult."

"When you were babysitting me, I always wondered what it would be like to kiss you," he admitted.

Her pulse jumped again, surprising her. "Now you know," she said quietly.

Another woman would have fished for a compliment, or coyly asked how she measured up. But that wasn't Claire, he thought. He found that oddly comforting.

"Yes," he said just as quietly. "Now I know."

Chapter Eight

In the days that followed, the kiss preyed on her mind at moments when she least expected it.

In all honesty, she didn't know what up-ended her world more, that she, the former Sister Michael, had passionately kissed a man, or that the man was five years younger and someone she used to babysit.

Well, isn't this part of why you left the order? her mind demanded. *Because you weren't satisfied with your life, weren't fulfilled anymore, and you thought there was something more outside the strict ramifications of your life? Maybe this was it, maybe the male-female-marriage thing is what you ultimately want and need.*

All well and good in theory and on paper, Claire thought, absently staring down at the French toast she was making for her mother. The French toast that was, even now, swiftly on its way to becoming a cooled, thin brick. But reality had a whole different feel to it.

She was elated. She was upset. She was frightened of her own feelings.

In a word, she was confused.

Careful what you wish for, right?

Who would have ever thought that the first man she'd *ever* kiss would turn out to be Caleb McClain? She removed the French toast from the frying pan and put it on a plate. Reaching for the powdered sugar, she drizzled it over the toast.

Had she summoned the courage to walk away from her work in God's arena only to rob a cradle?

What was wrong with her?

And what in heaven's name was she going to do with all these strange, unidentified feelings zigzagging through her?

Was she so out of control that she had to jump up and seal her mouth to the first man she came in contact with in her newly reclaimed secular life? Granted, Caleb was the best-looking man she'd seen in a very long time, but looks had never been important to her. Ever. She never judged by what she saw, only by what she knew to be inside.

Inside, she silently jeered at herself. What had been "inside" at that point had been the crackle of chemistry, the spark of lightning traveling through her veins.

Moreover, she wanted it to happen again.

Oh God, how was she ever going to face him again?

Maybe she wouldn't have to. But that would mean turning away from Danny. And besides, avoiding Caleb was tantamount to running. She couldn't allow herself to do that. It wasn't her way.

Secular life wasn't any easier than life as part of the Dominican order, she thought with a heartfelt, inward sigh.

Margaret looked down at the plate her daughter placed before her. Drawing it to her, she reached for the maple syrup.

"You're awfully quiet this morning," Margaret commented, pouring a slender stream of syrup over the French toast. "Is something wrong?"

Claire took her own plate and brought it over to the table. "Wrong?" she asked in her best innocent voice, sitting down opposite her mother. "No. Why?"

Margaret cut a small piece from her serving. "Because you're usually so talkative and cheery, you make Chatty Cathy sound like she took a vow of silence."

The reference went right over Claire's head. "Chatty Cathy?"

A faraway, reminiscent smile filtered over her mother's lips. "A doll I used to have. You pulled the string at the back of her neck and Chatty Cathy would talk and talk."

"Hence the name."

"Hence the name," Margaret echoed. She studied her daughter's face. Something was wrong. She knew it, Margaret thought. She knew it would only be a matter of time. It had just taken longer than she'd initially assumed. "What's bothering you?" she asked for form's sake. Leaning over the table, she placed her hand on top of Claire's. They were now the same size. She could remember a time when Claire's hand was so small, hers could swallow it up. Margaret deliberately lowered her voice, as if whispers could somehow bank down the shame that she felt was attached to the words. "Are you having regrets about leaving the order?"

Claire looked down at the hand covering hers, thinking to herself how safe that same hand had once made her feel as it stroked her hair, or touched her cheek, silently conveying the thought that whatever adversity they had to face, they would get through it together. She loved this woman who didn't always see things her way, loved her with such fierceness.

Her mother was her first priority, Claire reminded herself. Anything else was merely a distant second.

Reclaiming her hand, she used it to wave away her mother's speculation.

"No, Mother," she assured her softly, "I don't regret leaving the order." She shrugged lightly, dismissing the matter. "I'm just having some adjustment problems."

Margaret guessed at the most logical cause for her daughter's troubled appearance. "Are the children giving you trouble?" When Claire eyed her quizzically, she elaborated, "The class you've taken over for that pregnant teacher. Are they giving you trouble?"

They had talked about the class, but only about the amusing events, nothing serious. She wanted to make her mother laugh, not be concerned.

Claire shook her head, a smile playing on her lips. Teaching the children at this school was a piece of cake when she compared them to the native children she'd taught in Africa. There she'd had to compete with the elements, the animals and, in some cases, parents who didn't want to have their children educated by an outsider.

"No, they're delightful. It's nothing, Mother, really." Claire followed up her statement with the largest smile she could manage. "Now eat your breakfast before it gets too cold."

"Too late," her mother murmured. However, she continued eating.

But it wasn't nothing, Claire thought silently. It was something. A huge something.

To you, the voice in her head insisted. *But not to Caleb.*

Because Caleb had remained out here, in the secular world, doing secular things. Like kissing and all the things that came after that. Like having a relationship. Most likely he'd had a great many relationships before he'd gotten married. For him what had happened was nothing out of the ordinary. She was certain that by now Caleb had probably forgotten all about the other night.

But she wouldn't, Claire thought in the next heart-beat. She was pretty sure it was hard forgetting the moment when you thought you were going to go up in a puff of smoke.

Claire glanced at her watch. Dear Heaven, how had it gotten so late? She needed to get rolling. Pushing her plate away, she rose to her feet.

Margaret looked at her in surprise. "You're not going to eat?"

Claire shook her head. "Not hungry." And it was true. She'd thought she could eat, but her stomach refused to unknot. All she'd managed to get down this morning was some coffee. And even that sat heavily.

Margaret watched her suspiciously, her mother antennae up. "You're not going to come down with bulimia, are you?"

Claire laughed. "Not to worry, Mother. Besides,

people don't 'come down' with bulimia. It's a condition that's usually developed by pubescent girls who want to be model-thin."

Margaret was not about to back off just yet. "Do you?"

There were no dissatisfied images flashing through her head when she looked at herself in the mirror, no critiques as to how her body could appear better. She was what she was and it was fine with her. She hadn't even put on any of the sexy undergarments that Nancy had gotten her. They were still nestled in the back of her bottom drawer, where they would most likely remain for a very long time. They didn't go with her self-image.

"Not in my wildest dreams. This is me, Mother. When I have I ever been swayed by a trend?"

"Never," Margaret admitted, but then she looked at her pointedly. "But things change."

Her mother was back playing that same one note, Claire thought. "Not some things," she assured her. "I'm just running a little late, that's all." She wiped her mouth with the napkin. The slightest hint of pink came off on it. She still hadn't gotten used to wearing lipstick. But she was getting there and she did like experimenting with makeup. Like a little girl let loose in her mother's vanity, she mocked herself.

"Be sure to call your doctor and reschedule your appointment for four o'clock," she reminded her mother. This was a new doctor, one who specialized in patients with leukemia and came highly recommended.

Margaret nodded her head, but she didn't appear happy about it. "It's just another doctor, Claire. I'm perfectly capable of going by myself."

"No one said you weren't, Mother," Claire replied diplomatically. She carried her plate and empty coffee cup to the counter. "I just want to make sure that there's nothing we haven't covered."

"Other than me when I die, no," Margaret replied cryptically. "I think everything's 'covered.'"

Claire paused and looked down at her sternly. "You're not going to die, Mother."

"Everyone dies, Claire."

"Granted," Claire allowed philosophically, "but that's someday. Not soon."

Margaret laughed softly. "Got a handwritten guarantee in your pocket?"

"As a matter of fact," Claire countered, kissing her mother's forehead, "I do." She picked up her purse and briefcase from where they were leaning against the wall. "Not in my pocket, actually, because He's still using stone tablets to write his words on and they're really heavy, but I've got it."

These days, that was the only thing she did pray about, that her mother's disease would go into a lasting remission. She didn't feel she had the right to ask for anything for herself.

She would have to hit all the green lights if she didn't want to be late, Claire thought, picking up her pace. "Now be good, have a good day and *call your doctor*. And afterward," she promised, "we'll go out to eat or do something special."

"Just having you home is special," Margaret said, surprising her.

Claire doubled back and gave her mother a quick, enthusiastic hug. "I love you, Mother."

"I love you, too," Margaret said as she watched her

daughter fly to the front door. She was gone in an instant. "I love you, too," Margaret repeated more softly.

Sitting in the unmarked vehicle, coming up on their third hour of surveillance, Caleb noticed his partner, Detective Mark Falkowski, shifting uncomfortably.

Maybe lunch wasn't sitting so well. There was still a faint scent of hot pastrami sandwiches within the interior of the car, but mercifully, it was fading.

In the last half hour, the sound of crinkling aluminum foil as it was removed from said pastrami sandwiches had been practically the only sound that was heard.

Ski had already tried to strike up a conversation three times since they'd parked here. "Y'know, my pet rock talked more than you did," Ski said.

If Ski was trying to make him feel guilty, he wasn't succeeding, Caleb thought. He didn't feel like talking. Even more than usual. Losing Jane had sent him to a dark place. Communication was not a part of it. Besides, if he started to talk, to think, he would have to deal with what had happened the other evening with Claire. And he didn't want to. Not yet, maybe not ever. The last thing he needed was more guilt.

Instead, he focused on the man they'd been tailing for several days now. Their quarry was a middle-of-the-ladder pimp who dealt in the flesh peddling of minors. He wanted to bring the man down so bad, he could almost taste it.

Unfazed, he glanced at Ski. "Maybe you should start bringing it along."

"Maybe."

Obviously frustrated, Ski blew out a breath and tried again. "Want to talk about what's wrong?"

Caleb gave him a dark look in response. When Ski continued to wait for some sort of reply, he bit off a "No," thinking that would be the end of it.

He underestimated Ski's stubbornness.

"Well, something's sure sticking in your craw," Ski complained.

Caleb glanced away, focusing on the building across the street, the one their quarry had disappeared into. "Maybe what's 'sticking' in my 'craw' is a partner who's giving me the third degree."

"It's not Danny, is it?" Ski asked, pushing the point. "He's not sick or in any kind of trouble, is he?"

The same stoic tone answered him. "No."

Ski was far from satisfied. "Would you tell me if he was?"

Caleb squelched his irritation and caught himself giving way to a glimmer of a smile instead. His partner was finally catching on. If he'd had his choice, he would have preferred to work alone. But as far as partners went, Ski wasn't half-bad. He knew the man always had his back and in the long run, that was the most important aspect of a partner.

The ability to mind his own business ran a close second.

"No."

Caleb did *not* want to talk about what was nibbling away at him at odd moments. That he was caught between feeling unfaithful to Jane and wanting to kiss Claire again. Definitely not something he was about to disclose to Ski. He already knew on which side the man would throw his vote.

He spared Ski a glance. "You just don't give up, do you?"

"You're my partner. What you feel affects the job."

The reply drew a scowl from Caleb. Never once had he allowed what he was feeling to spill out onto his work. Not even when he'd felt as if his very heart had been ripped out of his chest.

"When have I ever let anything interfere with the job?"

Realizing his error the moment he'd said it, Ski was ready for him. "I didn't say 'interfere,' I said 'affects.'" He paused, waiting. Again, Caleb said nothing. So Ski pressed the point home. "So then everything's okay with Danny, right?"

Caleb ground out the word. "Right."

"Then it's something else that's bothering you. Anything I can do?"

"Yes," Caleb said tersely. "You can stop asking questions."

Ski merely smiled in response. "I would if you told me what's wrong."

Why was he surrounded by people who wouldn't let things be? He'd always been a private person to some extent. In the last year, he'd all but become an emotional hermit. And still Ski wouldn't take the hint. "And I would if it were any of your business."

If he thought that would make Ski back off, he was sorely disappointed. Instead, Ski began with round two.

"Okay, we've officially established that there is something wrong," he declared with a note of triumph. Obviously noting that Caleb was about to say something and judging that it was probably unflattering, Ski was quick to counter, "And for your information, since you're my partner, your business *is* my business." Pausing, Ski thought for a moment. "It's not the anniversary of Jane's death, that was a month ago." Caleb looked at him sharply. "I keep track of these things," Ski informed him in a tone that told Caleb that Ski shared his pain whether he wanted him to or not. "Is it that? Are you still having trouble moving forward? Did something happen to make you ambivalent about staying in place?"

In response, Caleb laughed dryly as the wheels in Ski's head turned faster.

"Or, are you moving forward and *that's* what's bothering you?"

The last guess was way too close. It caught Caleb off guard, and he stared at his partner in surprise before he managed to slip his poker face back into place.

The moment's hesitation was all that Ski needed.

"That's it, isn't it? You met someone, did something, felt something," Ski declared, honing in. "Oh, c'mon, McClain, I'm right and you know it. Help me out here."

Caleb remained unmoved. "You're not doing too badly on your own."

Ski leaned back in his uncomfortable seat. "You felt something," he repeated. He rolled his small brown eyes heavenward. "Hallelujah. Yes, Virginia, there is a Santa Claus."

"I don't know about Santa Claus," Caleb said in measured, even tones that were still fear-inspiring, "but there's not going to be a you if you don't start backing off beginning right now."

"I'll wear you down, you know. Like a steady stream of water hitting against a rock, I'll wear you down."

The door of the building across the street opened and their target exited, holding a briefcase that, from the way he was carrying it, seemed heavy. Caleb instantly sat up, alert.

He hit Ski's shoulder with the back of his hand as if to pull him out of a self-induced trance. "Okay, 'Water,' looks like we're on. Time to do what they pay us to do."

The questions vanished; Ski's expression hardened. Right before Caleb's eyes, his partner transformed into one of Bedford's best vice cops again.

The Silhouette Reader Service—Here's how it works: Accepting your 2 free books and 2 free mystery gifts places you under no obligation to buy anything. You may keep the books and gifts and return the shipping statement marked "cancel". If you do not cancel, about a month later we'll send you 6 additional books and bill you just $4.24 each in the U.S. or $4.99 each in Canada. That's a savings of 15% off the cover price. It's quite a bargain! Shipping and handling is just 50¢ per book.* You may cancel at any time, but if you choose to continue, every month we'll send you 6 more books, which you may either purchase at the discount price or return to us and cancel your subscription.
* Terms and prices subject to change without notice. Prices do not include applicable taxes. Sales tax applicable in N.Y. Canadian residents will be charged applicable provincial taxes and GST. Offer not valid in Quebec. All orders subject to approval. Books received may not be as shown. Credit or debit balances in a customer's account(s) may be offset by any other outstanding balance owed by or to the customer. Please allow 4 to 6 weeks for delivery. Offer available while quantities last.

▼ If offer card is missing write to: Silhouette Reader Service, P.O. Box 1867, Buffalo, NY 14240-1867 or visit: www.ReaderService.com ▶

NO POSTAGE
NECESSARY
IF MAILED
IN THE
UNITED STATES

BUSINESS REPLY MAIL
FIRST-CLASS MAIL   PERMIT NO. 717   BUFFALO, NY

POSTAGE WILL BE PAID BY ADDRESSEE

SILHOUETTE READER SERVICE
PO BOX 1867
BUFFALO NY 14240-9952

Send For
2 FREE BOOKS
Today!

I accept your offer!

Please send me two free *Silhouette Special Edition*® novels and two mystery gifts (gifts are worth about $10). I understand that these books are completely free—even the shipping and handling will be paid—and I am under no obligation to purchase anything, ever, as explained on the back of this card.

335 SDL EYMF   **235 SDL EYR3**

Please Print

FIRST NAME

LAST NAME

ADDRESS

APT.#   CITY

STATE/PROV.   ZIP/POSTAL CODE

Visit us online at
www.ReaderService.com

Offer limited to one per household and not valid to current subscribers of *Silhouette Special Edition*® books.

Your Privacy —Silhouette Books is committed to protecting your privacy. Our Privacy Policy is available online at www.eHarlequin.com or upon request from the Silhouette Reader Service. From time to time we make our list of customers available to reputable third parties who may have a product or service of interest to you. If you would prefer for us not to share your name and address, please check here ☐.

▶ Detach card and mail today. No stamp needed. ▶

S-SE-07/09

Chapter Nine

Caleb really wasn't sure why he drove by Claire's house. Maybe it was because Claire had aroused something within him, something that bore a passing resemblance to a glimmer of feeling. Or maybe it was nostalgia. A longing for the time when life was simpler and still full of promise. Promise he could, in his naiveté, believe in.

The trip down memory lane was almost involuntary, set off because Claire was living in the same house she'd lived in twenty-two years ago, the same neighborhood.

His old neighborhood.

He'd driven Jane here once, when she'd insisted on seeing where he'd grown up. She was pregnant with Danny at the time. He hadn't been back since.

This old house looked different now, he thought as

he slowed down. Someone with no taste had painted the outside a startling shade of rust with deep yellow trim and the owners had had some remodeling done on it. The house seemed wider, like a squatting rabbit, and the balcony on the second floor was gone. The space had been used to increase the footage of the room that used to lead out onto the balcony.

A pity, Caleb mused. He could remember standing up on his toes, leaning over the balcony railing and looking up at the stars.

Stars had been forfeited for extra space. Didn't seem like a trade-off to him.

Most of the houses, he noted as he continued to drive, had all had some sort of work done. New roofs, additions, expansions, new driveways. Landscaping that looked bright and fresh.

But not Claire's.

He eased his foot off the gas pedal as he came closer to the building. When he'd dropped her off the evening he'd come to her rescue, he really hadn't taken stock of her house. For one thing, it had been dark, for another, he was overdue home. But now that he looked at it, he could see that at least several things needed to be done. At the very least, the house was in dire need of repainting.

Caleb wondered why it had been allowed to fall into disrepair. Claire wasn't the type to let things slide.

And how did he know that? How did he know what her "type" was? He hadn't seen or heard from her since she was in her teens. People changed over the years.

God knew he had.

For once, his radar failed him. Caleb didn't realize

that the cherry-red Mustang was behind him until the vehicle passed by, pulling up into the empty driveway.

Claire.

He'd lingered just a moment too long, he realized, annoyed with himself. It was too late to turn around and go. The expression on her face as she got out of the car told him that she'd seen him.

Claire called something out to him, but he couldn't hear her. His windows were rolled up and the radio was on. It was on too low for him to actually make out the words, but there was a low hum being emitted. He turned it off. When he glanced up, Claire was crossing to him, mimicking someone rolling down windows. She eyed him expectantly.

Cornered, he obliged her.

"Lost?" she asked pleasantly, bending down so that her face was level with the open window.

When she'd come up behind him, she thought that her eyes were playing tricks on her. She really hadn't expected to see Caleb for a long time, not after he'd been so vulnerable with her. And certainly not after they'd kissed.

She'd hoped to see him, but she certainly hadn't expected to. She wondered if this was God's way of testing her—or was He being nice?

In either case, Caleb was here. Further proof that she didn't understand the male of the species.

Caleb shrugged. He wasn't accustomed to explaining himself. "Just thought I'd take a look at the old neighborhood in broad daylight."

Well, she supposed that made sense. Suddenly, she felt a little foolish for thinking that she might have had something to do with his appearance. She was giving

herself way too much credit. Was this what it was like
in the secular world? A thousand insecurities plaguing
you at every turn?

"What's your verdict?" she asked.

"It's changed some." He glanced toward his former
house. "Not always for the better." And then he nodded
toward her house. "Looks like yours could stand to
have some work done."

He watched as amusement bloomed on her lips and
in her eyes. Watched and felt a rustling within him that
should have remained dormant. And yet, he couldn't
quite put a lid on it. Or look away.

"So now you're given to understatements." Claire
glanced over her shoulder again. She viewed the house
with love, but she wasn't blind to its shortcomings. "It
could stand to have a *lot* of work done. Unfortunately,
with just a teacher's salary to work with, it's going to
have to wait a while longer." She didn't add that right
now, any excess money went toward medical bills.
Her mother had a small insurance policy, but there
were huge gaps in what it covered and what the actual
bills were. Even though the oncologist and the hospital,
Blair Memorial, had reduced their charges, the bills
were still staggering. "I'm just hoping that the roof
holds up through the rainy season."

The rainy season was still a couple of months
away, but when it decided to hit—and there had been
several dry years in a row—it could happen anytime
from November through March. He could remember
one February when Bedford was all but an island
unto itself for several days. It had rained so hard the
five-gallon trees his father had planted in their backyard the previous summer all went down beneath the

lashing rains. He and his parents worked all day getting them back up and staking them into the ground.

Since he was here, Caleb thought, he might as well get out. Doing so, he shoved his hands into his back pockets and took a closer look at the house. To cut costs, he'd done all the repairs and updating when he and Jane had bought their house. It had been a learn-as-you-go experience, but eventually, he got the hang of it.

"Shouldn't be that expensive just for the materials," he finally said.

"No," she allowed, "but the men who know what to do with those materials are."

He turned to look at her. "I'm not."

Caleb's response surprised not only Claire but himself, as well. He hadn't known he was going to make the offer until the words were out of his mouth.

Claire recovered before he did. She watched him uncertainly. "Are you volunteering to become my handyman?"

It was a teasing remark which she expected him to wholeheartedly deny. He was probably just saying that he'd fixed his own roof or something like that. No way was he saying what she thought he was saying.

Or was he?

Despite the fact that she'd left the order, she still believed that God watched over everyone, still believed in miracles. After all, she was hoping for one for her mother, wasn't she?

She saw Caleb shrug, as if it was no big deal. "Why not?" His hands still in his back pockets, he walked the front length of her house, carefully studying its condition. "I could fix your roof, replace some shingles, maybe give the place a face-lift with a new coat of paint."

He turned to look at her as if the ball was now in her court.

"Are you waiting for me to say yes?" she asked incredulously.

There wasn't even a hint of a smile on his lips. "That would be the next step, yes."

She was touched by the offer. It proved to her that she was right about him. The warm, sweet boy she'd known was still inside the brooding man. But she also knew she had to turn him down. It wouldn't be fair to take advantage of him.

"Caleb, you have a job and a son. You don't have time for this."

"Yes or no?"

"Yes," she said breathlessly.

"Okay. Unless something comes up, I'm usually off on weekends. I'll get started Saturday on the roof first, then we'll see about the paint job."

He left her speechless. It took her a second to recover. "But I can't pay you," she protested.

"Did I ask you for money?"

"No."

"Okay, then." Caleb rested his case. Turning on his heel, he started to walk back to his car. "Saturday," he repeated.

He was almost to the car when she called out, "Bring Danny."

That stopped him dead in his tracks. Certainly he'd misheard. "What?"

She crossed to him. "Bring Danny. I don't want

him missing out being with his father because you're helping me."

What was she thinking? "He'll just get underfoot," he told her. "And be bored."

"I seem to remember your father bragging about what a help you were—and you beaming in response." She grinned fondly, remembering. "Sunniest smile I ever saw. I think Danny could use some of that kind of reinforcement." She looked at him pointedly. "Don't you?"

He didn't answer immediately. Instead, he studied her for a long moment. Had he missed something? "How did this turn out to be about him?"

"Because everything's intertwined," she told him cheerfully. "You know that."

No, he thought, he didn't. Otherwise, why did he feel so adrift all the time?

But out loud he muttered, "If you say so," as he got back into his car.

Served him right, he thought darkly as he started up his car. That old saying was absolutely true. No good deed ever went unpunished. He'd felt sorry for her, made an offer and somehow, he'd gotten roped into not only doing repairs—by his own volition—but into bringing Danny along, as well.

Maybe it wasn't such a bad idea after all, he decided, thinking it over. If he brought Danny along, he had a feeling that Claire would keep him company. And that would be good for the boy. Danny seemed happy when she was around and she was a hell of a lot better for his son than he was in his present condition.

He glanced up into the rearview mirror and saw Claire still standing there, watching him go. Though he tried not to let it, the warm smile on her face remained with him all the way home.

And even longer than that.

"Your faucet could stand to be replaced," Caleb said matter-of-factly.

It was yet another Saturday and he was in her kitchen, getting himself a glass of water. In the last four weeks, he had begun to make himself at home here, not just at her behest—he figured she was just being polite—but as the work he did for her made him more and more familiar with the layout of the house.

Caleb drained the glass. For October, it was damn dry. And hot. The sweat he'd worked up was now sticking to every part of him. He needn't have hurried with the repairs on the roof. All indications pointed to it being another dry winter.

Claire took the glass from him and filled it. She could have used some water herself, she realized because, at the moment, she was trying not to notice how the sweat had his T-shirt adhering to every ridge on his body.

Not noticing wasn't going very well.

She found herself *really* looking forward to weekends. So much so that she took more care in dressing on Saturdays and the occasional Sundays than she did the rest of the week. The rest of the week didn't have her debating over which tiny, flirty bras and panties to wear. She'd finally dipped into the cache of undergarments that Nancy had gotten for her. Just having them against her skin made her feel more feminine. Made her feel prettier.

The first time she put them on, she silently upbraided herself for acting so adolescent. After all, it wasn't as if he was going to actually *see* any of this attire. But now, she looked forward to the selection process, to feeling like a woman. "Sister Michael" was becoming more and more of a distant memory.

When she offered the refilled glass back to him, he shook his head. Then, to her utter surprise, Caleb stripped his T-shirt off and shoved as much of it as he could into his back pocket. It hung there, trailing down like an oversize grey bandanna.

Claire forced herself to tear her eyes away and look at the sink, with its hairline crack running through the length of it. Another thing that could stand replacing.

Her throat was suddenly incredibly dry and her heart skipped beats.

"Are you moonlighting as a salesperson at the Home Emporium?" she managed to get out, silently congratulating herself on not losing her ability to speak.

"Just stating facts," he replied. He moved closer to her, bringing a wave of heat along with him that he seemed to be oblivious to. But she wasn't. "Your sink could stand to be replaced, too, but you probably already know that."

Take a deep breath. This is Caleb. Caleb, the little boy you babysat. Try to remember that. Yeah, right. Caleb, the little boy whose anticipated appearance makes you put on sexy underwear.

Get a grip, she ordered herself.

Easier said than done.

She cleared her throat. It just felt dryer, as if she'd just ingested a mouthful of sawdust.

"Most of this house could stand to be replaced," she

finally managed to say. She shrugged, focusing on the topic and not his biceps. He'd been such a skinny little kid, how had all this happened? "Dad died and then I left home. Mom went to work to pay the bills and keep herself busy." She looked around the kitchen. Nothing had been done to it for as far back as she could remember. "She didn't much notice anything at home, I guess. As long as the house was standing and it was neat inside, well, that was okay with her."

She sighed, remembering the last visit to her mother's doctor. How she'd held her mother's hand during the chemo treatment, her own heart breaking. From the bottom of her soul, she wished she could take this disease on in her mother's place.

"And now there are more important things for her to concern herself about," she concluded.

Caleb turned away from the sink. He looked at her for a long moment. "You mean the leukemia."

Claire inclined her head. "That, and the fact that my mother firmly believes that she's guilty of causing my divorce." She raised her eyes to his. "She thinks that God is going to punish her for that."

"Divorce?" he repeated. Had he missed something? "I thought you were—" He paused for a moment, trying to remember the phrase she'd used. "A Dominican Sister."

"I was," she told him. "That made me a 'bride of Jesus.' My mother thinks that the only reason I left the order was to be close to her in case she needed me. In her mind, that makes her guilty of being instrumental in bringing about my 'divorce.'"

He knew he should be getting back to work. But the more Claire talked, the more she drew him in. He couldn't make himself just ignore her and walk away. Besides, he was curious about something. Maybe it was a good sign.

And then again, maybe not.

"I thought that was why you left the order, to take care of your mother."

She shook her head. "No, that was just the catalyst that finally pushed me to do something. Truthfully, I'd been at a crossroads for a while before that." She saw no point in telling him about the children and the plague that had senselessly taken them away. He obviously had little faith to spare; sharing something that might just strip him of it entirely wouldn't be right. "I joined the order because it felt right. I left when it stopped feeling that way."

He supposed that made sense. As much sense as anything else. Caleb realized that he was staring at the way the sun seemed to be frosting strands of her hair, giving them golden highlights. He pulled himself back, silently upbraiding himself.

"And does it feel right now? Your being a teacher?" he added when she didn't answer him right away.

The smile that curved her mouth was slightly embarrassed, as if he'd asked something she wasn't prepared to answer yet.

"I'm still 'feeling' my way around," she admitted, the dimple in her cheek deepening as she emphasized the play on words.

In the distant background, he heard his son laughing. When they'd first started coming over, Claire had put Danny together with her mother, a match he wouldn't have attempted. But somehow, it was working. At least for Danny. The boy seemed happier lately, more like his old self. He was grateful to Claire for that. Grateful that someone could be there for his son while he was still wrestling with his demons.

"Well, I think you made the right choice," he said, straightening and moving away from the sink.

There it was again, that skipped beat. What was wrong with her?

"You're all Danny talks about," he continued, "and you're not even his teacher."

There'd definitely been a change in the boy. And, now that he thought about it, maybe there had been one in him, as well, however small. It had begun taking root four weeks ago, when he'd started coming by on his days off to work around her house. He'd meant to do only one thing, maybe two. But undertaking repairs here was a little like opening Pandora's box. It seemed for every repair he completed, two more would suddenly materialize. From where he stood, it was close to a never-ending chore. The house had been neglected for close to twenty-five years. That added up to a hell of a lot of repairs.

She wasn't about to take all the credit. Just as her mother's condition had been the catalyst to her finally taking action, her subtly maneuvering Danny had caused something else. She smiled at Caleb. Deep down, she'd known he would be a good father. A good man.

"Danny just needed some attention. From you," she underscored. "Your bringing him along to help has made a world of difference to him." She glanced toward the family room, where her mother and Danny currently were. The boy was teaching her mother how to play a video game. "Not to mention to my mother."

She owed him for that, Claire thought. Having Danny around had done far more for her mother than having her own daughter home. It was working out just as she'd hoped. Danny's budding, youthful enthusiasm had slowly gotten her mother to start looking forward to something again rather than morosely dwelling in the past, feeling as if the best of everything was now over.

"Well, you're the one who got me to bring him," he reminded her. "Until you insisted, I was going to leave him with Mrs. Collins."

"I didn't insist," she corrected amiably, "I 'suggested.'"

He gave her a look that all but pinned her to the wall. "You insisted."

She lifted a shoulder, letting it fall again. "This arrangement is better for everyone all around," she concluded.

Claire pressed her lips together. Her throat was still very dry and she was running out of places to look. Especially since she wasn't nearly as good at avoiding temptation as she used to be. Try as she might not to, her eyes kept straying back to his very bare, very sensual upper torso. Sweat had actually added a sheen to his body and the work he was doing had pumped up the muscles on his already toned arms and chest.

A person, even an ex-sister, could not look at that for long without having parts of her own body begin to dissolve.

She addressed her words to the air just right of his shoulder. "My mother still has some of my dad's things stored in the garage. Could I get you one of his shirts?"

Bemused, Caleb glanced down at his chest, then

back up at her. This was the way he always wound up when he was tackling a project. "Why?"

"No reason." Her voice sounded a little high. It struck her that that was probably the first lie she'd uttered since she couldn't remember when. "I just thought, since yours is wet, that you might just want to put on a dry one."

He saw no reason for her to go digging through some old, dusty box in the garage on his account. "No, this is okay."

Claire tried again. "Um, you'll probably get sun-burned," she pointed out. "The sun's getting pretty hot out there."

"I know. That's why I was sweating." He watched her, mildly amused. And then it dawned on him. Claire was trying very hard not to look at any region below his eyes. "Does my not wearing a shirt make you uncomfortable?"

She was about to deny it, but that would have been another lie. Two in the space of a couple of minutes was too much. One lie was bad enough.

"Oh God, yes."

The sensual rating, if there was such a thing, for the smile that slowly unfurled on his lips soared clear off the charts. Her pulse hammered all along her body as her breath moved like a slow, hot breeze through her lungs.

"Why, Sister Michael—" Caleb lowered his voice "—are you having impure thoughts?"

She said nothing. Instead, she began to turn away. While she still could. Because she suddenly had the most unruly urge to throw her arms around his neck and kiss Caleb.

"It's okay, you know," he called after her. "To have impure thoughts," he added in case she missed his point. "Because now that I mention it, I'm having them, too."

Chapter Ten

Claire stopped dead and then very slowly turned around to see if Caleb was just kidding or having fun at her expense.

But he wasn't.

Caleb seemed deadly serious, as if he actually meant what he said. Was he having impure thoughts about her? But how could he? He had to be joking. It would have been out of character for the man she'd come to know.

Wouldn't it have?

"I'm older than you are," she reminded him.

He eyed her incredulously, as if he couldn't believe that she'd actually said that.

"Hardly. When I was one and you were six, you were older. But now..." His voice drifted off as he shrugged carelessly.

Maybe the years meant nothing to him, but they did to her. She didn't feel old, but she did feel older than him. A lot older, even though, when it came to experience, she was a babe in the woods.

"But now I'm still five years older," she said pointedly.

He laughed shortly, shaking his head. "Doesn't mean anything anymore," he told her with the same careless attitude.

Caleb left her standing there as he went back to what he was doing. Strange sensations and longings moved through her, all of which were light-years away from what she was accustomed to feeling.

This was a whole new, exciting world for her. One she felt ill-equipped to face.

As a Dominican Sister, she'd always been very liberal in her thinking, in her attitude about people's behavior. She didn't believe in condemning people for acting on their feelings as long as love was involved rather than simply lust. But now that she was no longer part of the order, that sort of liberal thinking had suddenly deserted her.

At least as far as her own behavior was concerned.

There was no denying that being around Caleb stirred things up within her.

These unfamiliar feelings refused to go away and interfered with her work and her thought process. She had to get a grip.

She'd thought that once she left the order, things would be clearer for her. Instead, she became more and more confused.

And she had no idea where to turn for help. She couldn't turn to a priest because she'd supposedly turned her back on the lot of them. And conversations with God tended to be one-sided and not very conducive to problem-solving. Praying had not led to enlightenment.

If she talked to Nancy or Kelly, they'd cheer her on and take it as an invitation to start setting her up with any and every single male friend with a pulse. She didn't want that. And what she did want, she wasn't going to allow herself to want, she silently vowed.

The key to all this, Claire reasoned, was control. She was no stranger to that. Control had been at the heart of her last vocation. So she locked away her budding emotions as best she could and concentrated strictly on being there for her mother—making a point of getting her out of the house at least once a week—and being involved with her students.

But all the while, she found herself struggling to block out thoughts of a sweaty, gleaming torso and the man whose kiss had shaken up all her boundaries.

Doing so posed enough of a challenge when Caleb wasn't around. But when he was right there, working on yet another badly needed repair, it was next to impossible not to let her mind drift, nudging forth desires that had absolutely no place in her life to begin with, let alone centered around Caleb. She couldn't very well ignore him after he'd gone out of his way like this and literally come to her rescue time and again.

However, not to ignore him meant setting herself up for what amounted to slow torture.

"This is a test, right?" she murmured under her breath. She had a feeling she could probably do a lot better if the test involved locusts, not Caleb.

She had to get hold of herself, Claire silently insisted, and channel this into something positive. After all, she was clearly in debt to Caleb, not just for initially coming to her rescue at the restaurant, or for all the repairs he'd already done, but for the very fact that he had brought Danny along just as she'd asked.

She didn't even have to ask anymore, or remind him. Caleb brought the boy without being prodded. She took that as a good sign that things were slowly mending between father and son. She'd covertly watched as Danny had shyly volunteered to help with some of the repairs. Caleb had initially hesitated, but rather than send him away, he'd put a screwdriver in the boy's hand and began to show him what to do.

Danny had beamed and blossomed right before her eyes. From then on, he'd helped whenever he could. And when he wasn't "helping," he was keeping her mother company.

Having Danny around did wonders for her mother, forcing Margaret Santaniello to leave the depths of her depression and socialize with the boy who was just the right age, under other circumstances, to have been her grandson.

It had only been a few weeks and she was amazed at what a difference the time had made in her mother's life. It took more for life to thrive, to vanquish the strand of acute leukemia than just applications of chemotherapy. It took a positive attitude, a will to live.

By having Danny come around, by interacting with the boy, her mother had transformed from a woman who was stoically waiting to die to a woman who had something to look forward to. It was obvious that her mother avidly looked forward to weekends.

That makes two of us, Mother.

* * *

"I could have stayed with the order and just sent over Danny," she confided late one Saturday afternoon as she brought out a glass of ice water for Caleb. He was on the ladder, caulking the lower perimeter of one of the windows on the second floor. He wanted to make sure all the windows were impervious to rain before he painted the exterior of the house. His capacity for work took her breath away.

Pausing, Caleb looked down at her from his perch on the ladder.

"If you'd never left the order, Danny wouldn't be here," he said simply. Deciding to take a break, Caleb made his way down the ladder. Getting off, he accepted the glass and all but drained it in one long, parched gulp. "Besides," he reminded her, handing the glass back, "you said the reason you left is because you didn't feel the calling anymore, not just because your mother needed you."

"You were listening."

His shoulders moved in a careless shrug. He moved, she thought, like some kind of jungle cat.

You've got to stop noticing things like that.

"I'm a detective. It's my job to listen. And to remember details." He looked at her for a long moment. It wasn't impulse that had him saying what he said next. He'd thought about it, long and hard, and had decided to push forward. Because he found himself needing to see what would happen. "Go out with me tonight."

A cold shiver suddenly materialized, shimmying up and down her spine despite the heat of the afternoon sun. In the space of half a heartbeat, she went from confident to uncertain.

Maybe she'd heard wrong. "What?"

"I'm not speaking in tongues, Claire," he said patiently, never taking his eyes off her face. "Go out with me," he repeated.

There was sand in her mouth. It made her tongue unwieldy. "Where?"

"A restaurant, a walk, a movie. Doesn't matter."

She pressed her lips together. She needed home-team advantage, she thought. Besides, her mother would love the change of pace.

"Why don't you and Danny come over for dinner, then. Or just stay if you don't want to go home and then come back. I can whip something up—"

"Safety in numbers?"

She didn't know if he was insulted or amused. With Caleb, it was really hard to tell at times. But since he'd asked her a question, she could only be honest. "Something like that."

"All right, we'll stay." He glanced up toward the second floor, then back at her. "But eventually, you know, you and I are going to be alone together."

"We're alone right now," she said, her voice having more than a little difficulty emerging.

Caleb nodded. "All right."

She didn't quite understand. "All right?"

The question barely left her lips. Caleb framed her face with his hands and brought his lips down to hers.

And made everything else instantly vanish along with her halfhearted protest. Hot lava filled her veins as the kiss deepened. Claire felt something slipping from her fingers.

The sound of glass meeting concrete vaguely registered as she fell further and further into the inferno.

Leaning into it, into him, she wound her arms around his neck and for just a second, before she struggled to get her mind to kick in, she allowed herself to absorb the wondrously delicious sensations exploding all through her body.

This alone was worth leaving the order.

Guilt all but immediately followed, marring her pleasure.

"You can't keep doing that," she told him an eternity later, when she'd finally managed to get herself to break away and step back.

Amusement faintly curved his mouth. "Seven weeks between kisses hardly qualifies for 'keep doing that,'" he pointed out.

Seven weeks. He'd been keeping track. Why did that both thrill and frighten her at the same time?

She had no frame of reference to work with. This was a brand-new playing field for her.

"I'll—I'll go see about dinner," she murmured, backing away.

Caleb turned back to the ladder and began to climb back up. His mouth curved with amusement. "You do that, Claire."

Danny received with exuberance the news that he and his father were staying for dinner. "You make the best dinners, Miss Santaniello," he freely declared.

Her mother, however, tried to demur when she told her about guests for dinner. "I'm too tired to sit at the table, making conversation," she told her. "I'll just take something to my room."

Claire frowned. Maybe this was too much for the woman after all. The treatments her mother underwent left her feeling weak, but it had been almost a week since the last one. Her mother might just need some coaxing to stay. So be it. "Mother, please, I want you to stay."

"Don't you like us?" Danny asked, coming into the kitchen.

Embarrassed, Margaret cleared her throat. "Of course I like you, Danny, but I'm a tired old woman—"

"No, you're not," Danny protested.

"How would you know I'm not tired?" Margaret scowled.

"I don't. But I know you're not old."

Danny couldn't have said anything better if she'd personally written it down and given it to him to recite, Claire thought. Her mother was beaming.

"All right, I guess I can stay up for a while longer."

Danny took her hand. "You can sit by me."

"I would like that," Margaret told him.

Thank you, God, Claire thought as she turned to the refrigerator to see what she could come up with.

Dinner went wonderfully well. Caleb and his son stayed for the meal and then lingered awhile longer. Danny watched a cable channel devoted to cartoons with Margaret sitting beside him on the sofa. Caleb gruffly helped her clean up and put things away.

"He's really a very special boy," Claire told him, peering into the family room. Danny had his head on her mother's lap and from where she was standing, it looked as if the boy had dozed off. Her mother didn't appear that far from it herself. And there was a beautiful smile on her face.

"Yeah, he is a special boy," Caleb agreed. And,

much to his regret, he had been oblivious to his boy's sweetness. Until Claire had come along and taken charge. Things still weren't the way they used to be between him and Danny, but progress was being made. And he was trying, really trying, to make his way back from the island where he'd remained isolated for so long.

He owed her for that. For opening his eyes to how his suffer-in-silence behavior was actually affecting Danny.

The only way he knew how to repay Claire was to keep fixing things around her house. The way she had symbolically fixed things around his.

"I think it's time we got going," he told her, moving her aside and walking into the family room.

It tingled where he'd touched her. She tried her best to ignore it as she followed him into the room.

When she saw Caleb look stumped as to how to disentangle her mother from his son, she grinned. "Here, let me," she offered, keeping her voice low. Very gently, she eased the boy out from beneath her sleeping mother's protective hands and then picked him up. Turning, she presented Caleb with his sleeping son. "This is yours, I believe."

Their eyes met for a moment, and then he gazed down at the boy. "Yeah," he murmured, feeling a wave of love slowly move its way forward. "He's mine."

"I'll walk you to your car," she offered, striding ahead to open the front door. Behind her, her mother continued dozing as on TV a mouse in high heels and a frilly skirt squealed for her boyfriend to come save her. Again.

"I don't know how to thank you," Claire told him

once they were outside. "My mother's a whole new person. Danny's made a world of difference in her life."

Caleb pressed the button to release the security locks on his car. All four popped up and stood at attention. "And you've made a world of difference in his," Caleb countered. *And in mine.* He spared her a look before opening the rear passenger door. "One good turn deserves another, isn't that the expression?"

That didn't begin to cover it, she thought, but nodded. "Something like that."

Angling Danny in, he secured the boy in his seat and double-checked the seat belt cinches. They held. "Are you serious about wanting to thank me?" he asked as he closed Danny's door.

Why did it suddenly feel as if there were pins and needles dancing along her extremities? Where had all these nerves come from? "Yes."

He turned to face her. The moon was finally up and it seemed to give her a golden glow. She really was beautiful, he thought. Outside and in. "Then go out with me."

Shaken, she took him literally. "It's late and you've got Danny—"

He cut her off. She sounded as if she was about to pick up steam. "Not tonight, tomorrow night."

Wanting to say yes perhaps a little too much, she grasped on to the first excuse she could think of. "I've got papers to grade." It wasn't entirely true. All she had left was *a* paper to grade. That didn't exactly make for a huge stumbling block.

Unfazed, he said, "Grade them in the morning. Before we go out."

His eyes held her prisoner.

What would it hurt? To say yes, what would it hurt? she silently asked herself. After all, they were friends. She'd be going to dinner with a friend. It wasn't as if she didn't enjoy his company. She did. A great deal. Too much, maybe.

Blocking it, Claire took a breath and plunged ahead. Challenging herself. "All right."

He surprised her by laughing. She raised her eyebrow quizzically, waiting for an explanation.

"You look like a little kid in the doctor's office, bracing herself for a shot she knows is necessary," he told her. She was scared, he thought. That was okay. So was he. Scared, but curious. And intrigued. For the first time in a very long time, it didn't hurt to be alive. To breathe. He wanted to see if this was just a fluke. "I promise I won't sting."

That made her smile and relax again. "I know you won't."

Caleb got into his car and rolled down the window. "Tomorrow," he repeated. Turning on the ignition, he put the car in Reverse. "At seven."

Seven, she echoed in her head as she watched him drive away. She walked back into the house with goose bumps.

Caleb wouldn't tell her where they were going until they got there. "There" turned out to be The Belle of The Mississippi, a restaurant built to look like one of the riverboats that had traveled up and down the length of the Mississippi River two centuries ago.

This particular "riverboat" was docked at the harbor in Newport Beach. It offered a spectacular view of the water at night, complete with lights shimmering across the dark liquid surface.

It was like stepping back through a time portal into another world. Claire loved everything about it.

She forgot to be nervous.

"I didn't even know this place existed," she told Caleb over two hours later as they started to walk to his vehicle in the parking lot.

"It didn't when you lived here. You've been gone a long time," he reminded her. "There've been a lot of changes."

When she had lived here, more than half the developments hadn't even been built yet. But his comment made her think of him rather than a building boom. She slanted him a look as they walked. "Yes, there have."

Caleb could felt her gaze. His pulse accelerated just enough for him to notice.

He wasn't a man given to impulses. He was a man who planned things out, did things in a logical, pre-considered fashion. But this was different. This was stepping back into the past, doing things he'd thought about. Picking up opportunities that hadn't been there the first time around.

"Would you like to take a walk on the beach?"

She knew she should turn him down. She needed to be getting back. But it did sound like a lovely thing to do. *Go!*

"Okay," she agreed before she could change her mind. "But just a quick one."

He laughed. "I don't recommend jogging after the meal you just had." She had a healthy appetite. He liked that.

They walked to the back of the parking lot. A small path led onto the beach. A full moon cast its beams along the water. To the passing eye the beams seemed to lead right down to the path on the beach.

Stairway to Heaven, she couldn't help thinking.

As she removed her shoes and then picked them up by the straps, it occurred to Claire that the scene was made for lovers.

Caleb took her free hand. The moment he touched her, she felt her pulse speeding up wildly.

She had to stop this, she upbraided herself. This was Caleb, the little boy whom she'd read stories to. Why was she reacting to him this way?

"A penny for your thoughts."

Startled by the sound of his voice, she struggled not to show it. "Not worth that much, Detective."

To her surprise, he didn't drop the matter. "Tell me." He placed a penny in her hand. "I feel like splurging."

Her fingers closed around the penny. It still felt warm. Looking straight ahead, she said, "I was just thinking what a nice meal that was."

"Sister Michael, you're lying." His voice was filled with amusement.

Claire began to deny it, then decided not to compound the offense. "How did you know?"

"Your voice got deeper. It always gets deeper when you're not comfortable with what you're saying. And lying makes you uncomfortable."

Caleb stopped walking and dropped her hand. Then, as her breath lodged itself in her chest cavity, he turned toward her and burrowed his fingers in her hair. She could feel her heart hammering wildly now.

This was where she drew back, pulled away.

Stopped him. And yet, she found herself holding her breath, waiting. Yearning.

This wasn't fair. Not to him, or her. She didn't know who she was yet and he was the man with a broken heart.

"Caleb, don't," she whispered.

His eyes held hers. He knew he'd see the truth in her eyes. "'Don't' because you don't like it, or 'don't' because you do?"

She couldn't lie. "Because I do. And I shouldn't."

Right now, it wasn't about should or shouldn't, it was about need. "Why? Because you're an ex-nun?"

"Because I'm too old for you."

"You're five years older, not fifty," he pointed out. His eyes delved deep into her being. When he spoke, it was as if she could feel every word forming, brushing along her skin. "I don't think you understand, Claire. I haven't 'felt' anything except pain in a very long time. And I'm beginning to feel things because of you. Feel things *for* you. I don't see how that can be bad."

Oh God, he was saying all the right things. And yet, if she allowed herself to be swept away, that wouldn't be right.

Would it?

"It's not bad," she began, trying to make her way through the minefield. "It's just not—"

She ran out of words. But that wasn't why she didn't get a chance to finish. She didn't get a chance to finish because he was kissing her again.

Chapter Eleven

He took her breath away.

More than that, Caleb took her very will away. All she wanted to do, heaven help her, was melt into him. Because as the seconds ticked away and the kiss deepened, the rush she experienced grew wilder and more heady. It spurred her on, making her want more. She could feel a quickening in her loins, a desire filling her that she'd never experienced before.

Was this what it felt like to be a woman, without her habit or her vows to hide behind?

And then, just as suddenly as he had kissed her, he was drawing his mouth away from hers. But the heat, the fire still remained, still burned brightly. Still fueled the electricity that had sprung up within her.

Claire felt as if she was coming unglued. She didn't know if she could deal with any more uncertainty.

"You're making me afraid," she confessed in a small, husky voice.

That goes double for me, he thought. He'd been so confident that he'd never feel anything for anyone again. And yet, here she was, tapping into some hidden reserve that had been set up in her name several decades ago. *Afraid* didn't even begin to cover it.

But the uncertainty, the confusion in her eyes, got to him. Caleb lightly touched her face, wishing he knew what the hell he was doing here.

"No need to be afraid. I'll never do anything you don't want to do," he promised.

Claire shook her head, doing her best not to react to his touch, to the warmth of his hand against her skin. "No, you don't understand. I'm not afraid of you. I'm afraid of me. I'm afraid I'm going to wind up doing something that I shouldn't." There'd always been strict rules to follow. Now, she found herself not wanting to follow them. She raised her eyes to his. "This is all very new to me."

He framed her face, not to kiss her, but to make her look at him, look into his eyes and into his soul because he really believed that she could. "Then we'll take it very slow."

Her pulse raced. No, she couldn't start something now. Her mother needed her. And she still needed to sort out her head. This was just confusing matters, up-heaving everything she thought she believed in.

"We shouldn't take it at all," she told him, but her voice was far from firm, far from convinced.

His eyes never left hers. "Do you really believe that?"

Lying would have put an end to it. But she couldn't

lie. Maybe to herself, but not to him. Not when he looked at her that way.

She pressed her lips together and slowly moved her head from side to side.

"No."

A hint of a smile played on his lips. Or maybe that was just a trick played on her eyes by the moonlight. He said nothing. Instead, he just took her hand in his and began to walk back to the car.

Oh, Lord, she thought. *What am I doing here with him like this? What am I doing, period?* She was supposed to be less confused by now, not more.

Only silence met her mental query. Apparently God wasn't taking calls. She was on her own.

They said very little, allowing the radio to fill the silence that existed in the car. It wasn't an uncomfortable silence. Right now, empty chatter would have been far more uncomfortable. She needed time to think, to make order out of the chaos in her head. And yet, she knew that thinking wasn't the answer.

Some things you couldn't dissect. Some things just had to be.

And suddenly, in a sea of uncertainty, she knew what she had to do. As they made the turn that would eventually lead to her development, she looked at Caleb. She couldn't pretend any longer that she didn't feel something for him that went beyond friendship.

She'd left the order for a reason. To find her place in this secular world. She couldn't do that if she was hiding.

"Take me to your house," she said quietly.

Caleb's hands tightened on the steering wheel.

There was nothing he wanted more right at this moment than to take her. Here, at her house, at his. It didn't matter where. But he didn't want her to feel as if she was somehow coerced.

He slanted a glance at her. She had the face of innocence. "Are you sure?"

Claire took a deep breath before nodding her head. "I'm sure."

Caleb laughed. "I'm taking you home. Your home," he clarified in case she misunderstood him.

Stunned, she stared at his profile. "You're turning me down?"

He had no choice. "Claire, just now, when you said you were sure, you looked as if you were bracing yourself for the dentist to begin drilling on a cavity. That's not what it's all about." He knew she'd been a Dominican Sister for the last twenty-two years, but she'd had a life before she entered the order. "Don't you remember?"

Claire stared down at her lap. "There's nothing to remember."

For a second, her words didn't make any sense. And then it hit him like a runaway semi. "Are you telling me that you're a...?"

If she looked at him, would she see pity in his eyes? Sometimes she was just too honest, but there was no getting around her admission. She peered back through the windshield. The world seemed very dark.

"Yes."

"You never made love?"

"No."

That didn't seem to make sense. "But you were seventeen when you left."

He sounded so incredulous, she couldn't help laughing. "I was part of a silent majority. Not everyone was sexually active by seventeen." She had several friends who claimed to have abstained. "My sense of God and mother—not always in that order—was very strong. Besides, at the time I hadn't met anyone I wanted to be with. Before now," she murmured after a beat. Caleb wasn't saying anything, wasn't making any comments. She began to feel uneasy. And foolish. "Say something. Please."

"I'm overwhelmed." He glanced at her as he slowed at a red light. "I thought women like you were like unicorns. A myth." Everyone he'd known when he was that age was sexually active. He blew out a breath. "This puts a different spin on things."

Of course it did, she thought. What normal, red-blooded male at his age would want to make love with a thirty-nine-year-old virgin? He probably thought she belonged on display in the Smithsonian.

She continued to stare out the windshield. "I understand."

Caleb opened his mouth to stay something, then closed it again. Instead of speaking, he pulled over to the side and put his vehicle in Park.

"No," he told her, "I don't think you do. Being someone's 'first' is a huge responsibility."

"I won't be grading you." And then she shook her head, embarrassed at the flippant remark. "Sorry, that just slipped out." Maybe this was for the best. She had no business complicating his life like this. Besides, this went against everything she'd been taught. Good girls didn't have sex before marriage. That went for thirty-nine-year-old women, too.

"This was a bad idea. I don't even know why we're talking about it."

He continued just sitting there, the car idling. "Maybe because we can talk. There's something about you that makes it easy. There always was," he added, recalling times in his past. Then she had been an older, wiser woman. That had all been part of the crush he felt. Caleb put the car back into Drive. "C'mon, I'll take you home." But even before the words had left his mouth, his cell phone rang.

Caleb tensed. The life of a police detective was never a hundred percent his own. Unofficially, he was on call 24/7.

But when he glanced at the screen, he saw that the number belonged not to his partner or someone else at the precinct, but to his home. An uneasiness slithered through his stomach as he flipped opened the phone and put it to his ear. "Hello?"

"Caleb." There was a woman's voice on the other end of the line. He recognized it immediately. Mrs. Collins. "I thought you'd want to know that Danny fell off his bed and bumped his head." The woman sounded flustered and concerned. "I don't know if you want me to take him to the hospital."

He saw Claire looking at him, concerned. It took him a second to realize she was reacting to the expression on his face. Dire scenarios formed in his mind.

"Is he bleeding?" The moment the question was out of his mouth, he saw Claire stiffen.

"No, but—" Mrs. Collins's voice trailed off. "Maybe I'm overreacting. I'm sorry, Caleb. It just happened so fast—"

He made no comment. Blame was useless. He had

to get to his son. "I'll be there as soon as I can." With that, he ended the call, closing the phone and stuffing it back into his pocket. He put the car into gear again.

"Don't bother dropping me off," Claire told him. "Take me with you."

"Are you sure?"

"Caleb, I'm also a registered nurse," she reminded him. "I want to see Danny. If he's hurt, I can assess the situation better than you can."

He didn't argue. Grateful for the offer, he turned his car around and headed straight for home.

The moment Caleb unlocked his front door, Claire edged him out of the way and made straight for Danny. The boy was lying on the sofa.

Mrs. Collins, who from the top of her snow-white hair to the bottom of her sensible shoes looked like the personification of everyone's ideal grandmother, wrung her hands as she hovered in the background, offering a profusion of apologies.

"It just happened so fast," she cried. "One moment he was jumping into bed, the next, he was falling out the other side and there was this awful noise—"

"It wasn't so awful," Danny protested. He looked up at Claire. "I'm okay. Really," he insisted.

"That's a pretty big bump for okay," Caleb commented, far from reassured as he moved the fringes of dark hair away from his son's forehead.

Claire sat down on the sofa beside the boy, looking intently into his eyes. His pupils weren't dilated, which was a very good sign. "How many fingers do you see?" she asked, holding two up.

"Five," he answered. When she frowned slightly,

Danny leaned forward and touched each of her fingers, the ones that she held up, and the ones she kept down. "I see five," he repeated.

She laughed and hugged him. "Can't argue with that logic," she told him. Releasing Danny, she glanced over her shoulder at Caleb. "There's no concussion." He continued to appear dubious, so she added, "You can still take him to the E.R., but I think it's a pretty safe bet that the goose egg on his forehead is probably the worst of it. Do you have an ice pack?" she asked.

Caleb didn't answer. Instead, anticipating her next statement, he turned on his heel and went to retrieve it from the freezer section of his refrigerator. He was back in a minute, holding it out to her.

"This should help a lot," she told Danny, gently applying the ice pack to the lump on his forehead. "I want you to hold that there for a while, Danny. It'll take the swelling down. And don't worry," she told him, lowering her voice as if she was sharing a secret with him, "your hair'll cover it. Nobody has to know—if you don't want them to." She winked at him conspiratorially. In her experience, boys liked to show off their battle scars and brag about them.

"'Kay," he said solemnly. Then, as she began to get up, he caught her hand, winding his small fingers around hers. "Miss Santaniello, can you stay with me until I fall asleep?" he asked hopefully.

Caleb intervened. Claire had already gone out of her way. "She has to get home, Danny."

She saw the flash of disappointment in the boy's eyes. That was all she needed. "No, that's all right." She ran her hand ever so lightly over the top of the boy's head. "I can stay." Claire raised her eyes to meet

Caleb's. "Why don't you walk Mrs. Collins home while I get Danny into bed." Even as she made the suggestion, Claire picked the boy up from the sofa and began to head for the stairs.

Dumbfounded, it took Caleb a moment to come to. He jockeyed for position in front of her. "He's too heavy for you."

Claire shook her head, shifting so that Caleb couldn't take his son out of her arms. "I'm stronger than I seem," she assured him as she began to climb up the stairs. Danny snuggled against her.

"She's a very nice girl," Mrs. Collins commented, hiking her purse up on her arm as she and Caleb walked out the front door.

Claire heard Caleb murmur, "Yes, I know." She couldn't explain why, but a small thrill shimmied up and down her spine—even as she tried to tamp it down.

It took a while for Danny to finally drop off to sleep. At first they talked and Danny asked her questions about her evening. But when he asked her if she liked his father, she thought it was time to pull out a storybook.

"But do you like him?" he asked.

"Of course I like your father," she said, sitting down beside him with a book she'd selected.

"Why?" he demanded.

"Because he's a very nice man." The book was one that promised a story a night for the entire year. Perforce, the stories were all short, each just about covering the length of a page.

"He used to be nicer," Danny confided, leaning back against his pillow. "When my mama was around."

"It's been tough on both of you," she agreed. "And some people take longer to get over things. You have to give your dad a little more time."

"Could you stay here and be my mama?" Danny asked out of the blue. "He smiles when you're here."

"He'll smile when I'm not here," she assured him. "Just give him time," she repeated. "And love him."

"I do," he told her, struggling to stifle a yawn.

Claire began reading.

Three stories later, Danny had dropped off to sleep. Very carefully, she closed the book. Then, watching the boy's face for any sign that he was waking up, she made her way over to the bookshelf and replaced the storybook. She held her breath as she tiptoed out of the room.

Completely preoccupied with making a silent getaway, she didn't realize that Caleb was standing in the hall right outside Danny's room until she walked smack into him. She clamped down her lips, swallowing the startled sound that emerged. Her entire body went on red alert as her chest bumped up against his. Electric currents went shooting every which way from the point of contact.

She never said a word.

Instead, just this once, she allowed her instincts to take over, to lead her. A cauldron of emotions, hovering so close to the surface ever since the walk on the beach, boiled over. Her arms went around his neck.

He didn't seem to need any more encouragement. Caleb swept her into his arms, kissing her with such unbridled passion she thought she would ignite right there.

Or at least melt into a heated puddle.

He hadn't intended to do this. After dropping Mrs. Collins off at her house, he'd come upstairs to see how Danny was doing. But before he could enter the room, he heard them talking. It took him back to his own childhood. Back to when he was the one in bed and Claire was talking to him as if he were an adult, or so it had seemed at the time.

The warm feeling, mingling with relief that his son was all right, overwhelmed him. So he'd stood out there and listened as Claire and Danny talked. He was startled when Danny asked her to be his mother. That was when it really finally sank in. Danny missed his mother as much as he did.

He was about to go in, to say something to Danny in response to his son's request, but then Claire had begun reading to the boy. The moment was just too special to interrupt, but he couldn't force himself to leave, either. Because just standing out there and listening had somehow soothed his soul even as it took him back.

Gratitude welled up within him.

But the moment he saw her emerge from Danny's room, gratitude suddenly turned into something more. Something that he couldn't express verbally. So he did the next best thing: he acted on his feelings. And within less than a second, the pull between them had suddenly mushroomed and escalated.

Still kissing her over and over again, Caleb picked her up into his arms and made his way into his bedroom without saying a single word. Her arms tightened around his neck. He knew it was her way of saying yes.

Walking in, he shouldered the door closed, then crossed to his bed and placed her on top of the rumpled blue and white comforter. Claire gave no indication that she was about to release her hold on him so he went down with her.

The second their bodies touched, another, larger wave of heat, more urgent than before, flared over him. Consuming him. Caleb glided his hands along the outline of her body, caressing, absorbing, familiarizing himself with every curve, every line.

But even as his body turned into a smoldering inferno, he forced himself to draw back. If this wasn't what she wanted, *really* wanted, he had to let her back away. Even if it ripped him to shreds.

"Claire."

Oh, no, no, this wasn't the time for a dialogue, or for any words at all. If she practiced restraint, if she struggled to allow a cooler head to prevail, she knew she was ultimately going to regret it. Because this might never happen to her again. She'd lose her nerve if she thought about it. And she needed for it to happen. More than anything, she wanted to know what she had missed by stepping back from the secular world.

So she pulled him back down to her so that his lips moved against hers.

Claire shivered with anticipation as she felt his hands on her, her body straining against the confines of her clothes. And then, just like that, they weren't on anymore. He'd gotten rid of both her clothes and his.

For a moment, embarrassment found her, threatening to steal her away from experiencing the rush that was, even now, undulating its way forward, up through her chest. And then, embarrassment splintered like brittle glass, disappearing as larger, more ethereal sensations took hold of her.

Everywhere Caleb touched, he just managed to make her want him more. She had no idea that so much longing could fill one person. Every inch of her was on fire with passion and desire. She'd felt passion before—passion for her work, for a cause, but all that paled in comparison to what she was experiencing right at this moment. It was as if something wild surged within her, gaining strength and magnitude.

She could tell he was holding back and for that, she was grateful, because she wanted to savor each new sensation, to explore it and make it her own. She could have sworn swirling lights and fireworks spun in her head. It all took her breath away.

He took her breath away.

And then, he was over her, weaving his fingers through hers. "Look at me," he whispered against her temple. "Open your eyes and look at me."

Until he'd said it, she hadn't realized that her eyes were closed. Opening them, she looked up into his eyes, emotions racing through her at incredible speeds.

And then he entered her.

A shaft of pain shot through her, taking her breath away. She thought herself past it. She saw concern in his face and sensed that he was going to draw back. To shield her. She raised her hips and urgently thrust up against him, silently telling him that it was all right.

That it was *more* than all right. It was wonderful.

The next instant, a rhythm hummed through her as the pain receded. She moved to its tune. Moved with him until he brought her up to where she'd never been before. To the peak of the ionic storm, with each explosion larger than the last. She felt like laughing and crying at the same time. There seemed to be no end, no way to describe what was happening except that it was magnificent and she was at the center, hanging on for dear life.

Chapter Twelve

The rush, the euphoria that her first experience with lovemaking created and sustained, was absolutely incredible. Claire had always thought of herself as a down-to-earth person, but this had felt like an out-of-body experience. It definitely fell under the heading of a minor miracle. She'd had no idea it could be so incredibly pleasurable.

And even after it was over, as she slowly floated back to earth, she could hardly catch her breath. Her pulse hammered wildly and a plethora of feelings danced through her, mingling so that she couldn't focus on any one of them. Instead, she just enjoyed and savored them all.

Gradually, she became aware that her eyes were still closed. When she opened them, she saw that

Caleb had raised himself up on his elbow and was watching her.

Was he disappointed? Heaven knew she wasn't. If anything, she was magnificently overwhelmed. But he had experiences to compare this to. Did she come up sorely lacking? She wished she could read his expression, but couldn't. She only hoped that the experience didn't rank as a low point in his life.

Claire drew in a deep breath, then slowly let it out again. She willed herself not to sound breathless. And prayed that her voice wouldn't crack.

Her mouth curved. "Waiting for me to start casting out beams of light?"

Tenderness had been absent from his life. The seamy world he moved through every day in his line of work had hardened him, changing him from the lighthearted boy he'd once been. And Jane's death had wiped him out completely. But there was a faint stirring now, like the distant sensation of an itch existing on a surface that had previously been rendered totally numb.

He curbed the desire to lightly stroke her face. "Just want to make sure you're all right."

His sensitivity touched her more than she could possibly say. It tucked itself around all of her newly budded emotions like a soft, downy blanket. To her surprise—and relief—she felt no guilt. She knew it was just a matter of time. Having been raised to be "a good little girl" and having been a Dominican Sister to boot, sprigs of guilt were a way of life. But for now, she'd savor its absence.

Rather than guilt, she was confused. What she'd experienced had been so wondrous, and yet, she knew that she shouldn't have allowed it to happen. For a multitude of reasons.

If, perhaps now, a sliver of guilt was making its appearance, it was there because she'd enjoyed sampling this "forbidden fruit" so very much.

In a way, she almost felt as if she'd been reborn.

"I think," she told him, addressing his comment, "that I'm way beyond 'all right.' I think I'm hovering somewhere around 'fantastically incredible.'"

Amused, Caleb couldn't contain the soft laugh that escaped. This time, he did allow himself to run his knuckles against her cheek. He watched as emotions seemed to blossom in her eyes.

"Yes," he agreed, "you were."

Claire sighed, taking stock, trying to find her way back to a point she was familiar with. It wasn't easy and she didn't give this feeling up willingly. There were still the remnants of shooting stars darting to and fro within her. And her body was tingling, especially at the very center. *Orgasm* was far too plebian a word to describe what she'd experienced. She continued to hug the sensation to her.

And then, slowly, it dawned on her what Caleb had just said. That he wasn't disappointed with their lovemaking. Wasn't disappointed with her hopelessly novice attempts to give him back a little of the pleasure he'd created for her.

She looked at him in surprise. "Really?"

"Really." He had an urge to kiss her again, and to just hold her to him. Nothing more, just hold her.

As the thought sank in, he froze.

That was the way it had been with Jane. He'd loved

just holding her in his arms. How could he be replacing her so soon? What was the matter with him?

Claire saw the change in his face immediately. "What's wrong?"

"Nothing." He'd nearly snapped the answer out, but stopped himself at the last moment. He was angry at himself, not her.

"'Nothing' brought a dark look into your eyes," she told him. Tugging, she brought the comforter up around her and covered herself with it. She sat up and looked at him. The moment was gone. She was his friend again, with a little of Sister Michael on the side. "There's no reason to feel guilty."

Caleb looked at her sharply, an annoyed retort on his lips, framed in denial. It died soundlessly. There was no point in lying. He *did* feel guilty. Which struck him as ironic, considering the circumstances. "I should be the one saying that to you."

"Yes," she agreed. "You should."

But she wasn't going to deal with the tiny slivers of guilt that were beginning to prick her, at least, not right now. She could only deal with one thing at a time and he needed her. So she sublimated her own needs, her own insecurities, concerns and fears that started to push forward, in order to help him with his.

"Jane wouldn't have wanted you to feel guilty." She saw the brooding look descending over him. He didn't like her invading personal territory. *Too bad.* It was what friends did for each other. "Danny told me some things about his mom and she sounds like she was a wonderful person."

Why did the mere mention of her name still hurt so damn much? "She was."

She wanted to hold him, to comfort him. But she knew where that would lead. They needed to talk now. So she knotted her fingers together in her lap and prayed that she hadn't lost the ability to talk someone into feeling better about themselves.

"Wonderful people don't want the people they love to go into hiding, to mourn them for the rest of their own natural lives. Jane would have wanted you to be happy," she told him in a quiet, firm voice. "To be there for Danny and find your way out of the darkness."

"Is this what you did as a nun?" he asked. "Give pep talks, try to make people feel better?"

The habit and her vows had nothing to do with her inherent desire to help others. But it was why she'd deliberately chosen an order that wasn't cloistered, the Dominican Sisters as opposed to the Dominican nuns.

She wasn't the type to silently do penance for the rest of the world, locking herself away from that same world. She was far too active for that kind of life, too concerned about helping people heal both physically and mentally to hang back and leave it all up to God to do on His own. Sometimes, He liked a little help. They'd been a kind of team once, she recalled. Maybe, in a way, they could be one again.

"This is what I did as me," she told him. "What I do as me," she added. She offered him a smile. "Usually, I'm fairly successful."

He laughed shortly. She was persistent, if nothing else. "I bet you are."

Claire shifted, still keeping the comforter tucked tightly around her. She could feel it slip along her back, but that couldn't be helped. The awkwardness of the situation was beginning to penetrate.

Claire raised her chin, a touch of pride entering her voice. "I'd better go."

This was where he should say "Yes, fine." And yet, he realized that he didn't want her to go. He wanted her to stay. With him. Damn, but there was no end to his confusion. "You can stay the night."

"But you'd rather I didn't," she guessed. It wasn't difficult to read the ambivalence in his eyes. She took no offense. This had been a big step not just for her, but for him, as well. "That's all right," she added quickly when she saw he was struggling with a denial, "I've got to get back to my mother before she becomes convinced that I've taken a nonstop express elevator into hell. Besides, I'm sure Nancy's gone home by now."

Caleb nodded. Maybe this was for the best, after all. Reaching for the jeans he'd discarded on the floor, he swiftly slid them on. Finding his shirt took a bit of doing. Somehow, it had been kicked under the bed. He shook it once to get the dust off it, then slipped it on.

"I'll drive you home," he announced.

He probably didn't realize why he couldn't do that. She smiled, shaking her head. "That's all right, you stay here with Danny. I can call a cab."

Danny. He'd almost forgotten about the boy. That had never happened before, no matter what his state. Damn, but he was addled tonight. She was right, of course. He couldn't just leave the boy asleep in his bed. That would have been the height of irresponsibility.

Caleb nodded as he dragged an exasperated hand through his hair. "If you don't mind…" He had no idea how to end his sentence.

Wearing the comforter around her like a bulky Roman toga, the clothes she'd gathered together pressed against her chest, Claire paused just before the bathroom to smile at him.

"I don't mind," she assured him. "Besides, I'd be worried about Danny being alone."

It was only a ten-minute run to her house. Twenty for a round trip. But she was right, Danny couldn't be left alone. What if the boy woke up while he was out and needed him? It was too late to rouse Mrs. Collins out of bed and ask her to watch Danny even though she'd said she was available anytime, day or night. He saved those times for when he was called away to the job in the wee hours of the night.

Shoving his hands into his pockets, he waited for Claire to emerge from the bathroom. When she did, he gave her the name of a local cab company. She made the call and he walked her downstairs. Then accompanied her to the front door when the cab arrived some ten minutes later.

"Look in on Danny from time to time tonight," she advised. She was just giving him medical advice. Why was her heart pounding again? And why was she fighting an urge to kiss him one last time? Without realizing it, her voice was picking up speed. "And if he throws up, take him to the Emergency Room immediately. And when you get there—"

He shoved his hands deeper into his back pockets, knowing if they were free, he'd be pulling her to him. As an added deterrent, he reminded himself that the cab driver was watching them. The urge wouldn't go away.

"Yes?"

She ran her tongue along her lips, trying to moisten them. They felt bone-dry. As dry as her throat did. "Call me and I'll come down right away."

"Why? What could you do then?"

"I could hold your hand and tell you it was going to be all right."

He almost let her go. And then, just as she turned away from him, he caught her by the waist, turning her back toward him.

And kissed her one last time. Even though the cab driver was watching.

The effects of Caleb's last kiss still lingered sweetly in Claire's mind and on her lips as she walked through the door of her house fifteen minutes later.

She was going to have to find a way to deal with that, Claire told herself. Later. Right now, she just wanted a few more minutes to enjoy it.

Considering the late hour, she fully expected the house to be silent and dark. Margaret Santaniello had never been a night owl, preferring to go to bed by ten at the latest, if not earlier. Her father used to tease her mother about that, saying that if he hadn't had her, Claire, to pal around with, he would have been a lonely man. She and her father watched old movies aired by one of the local stations, but mostly, they talked. About everything.

She caught herself missing him, even after all these years. The moment she did, she instantly felt for Caleb. His wife had only been gone a little more than a year. How raw was his wound?

A faint bluish light emerged from the family room, along with the low drone of voices. Did her mother have company? At this hour? She found it highly doubtful. There wasn't any other car in the driveway. Her mother was alone.

So then who…?

As she pocketed her key and walked in farther, the drone turned into audible dialogue. Or rather, a monologue. Someone touted the services of a local florist.

A commercial.

The television set was on. Curious, Claire walked into the family room. And then she smiled to herself. Her mother was on the sofa, sitting before the TV. The remote control was dangling from her fingers, a hair's breadth away from falling on the floor.

Margaret Santaniello was sound asleep.

Looking at her, Claire shook her head. "I'm too old for you to wait up for, Mother," she chided softly.

As gently as she could, she removed the remote control from her mother's lax fingers and put it on the coffee table. Closing the TV, she took the large, soft gray throw that resided on the back of the sofa and spread it over her mother, covering her. It wasn't cold, but the temperature tended to drop in the predawn hours. She didn't want her mother catching a chill on top of everything else.

"No, you're not," Margaret answered, opening her eyes and causing Claire's heart to leap into her throat. "There's no set cut-off point where you stop being a mother. In for a penny, in for a pound," she added. Yawning, she rotated her neck. It had obviously grown stiff in that position. "So," she asked, looking at Claire, "how was it?"

Guilt had her freezing. They said that some mothers were very intuitive when it came to their children, no matter what their age. Her mother couldn't possibly tell how her evening had wound up.

Could she?

"'It?'" Claire asked, hoping that she sounded sufficiently innocent.

Her mother gave her an odd look, as if she didn't quite understand her reaction. "Dinner. You went out with Caleb for dinner, didn't you?"

Thank God she didn't suspect. "Yes, I did."

Margaret looked at her watch, angling it slightly in order to make out the numbers. It was an analog watch given to her by her husband on her wedding day. "You must have had really slow service."

"Mrs. Collins called just as we finished eating and Caleb was about to bring me home," Claire began to explain, grateful that she could fall back on the truth. "Danny hit his head. I insisted Caleb take me to his house so that I could make sure that Danny was all right."

It seemed to her that her mother was looking at her very closely. "And was he?"

"Yes. It was just a bump. A rather big one, actually." Offering her mother her arm, she helped get the older woman to her feet. "But I stayed around just to make sure that everything was all right and that he didn't suddenly pass out or start throwing up. Danny asked me to read him a story before he went to bed. You know how that goes...." She let her voice trail off.

Margaret nodded, still looking at her. "And he fell asleep just now?"

"No, a while back." She knew her mother was waiting to find out why it had taken her so long to get home. "After that, Caleb and I...talked," she finally said, vacillating between telling her mother the truth and seeking the shelter of a lie. She decided that her mother had enough to deal with as it was. If Margaret

Santaniello thought that her daughter was making love with someone, especially a younger man, that just might send her over the edge. Better a small "untruth" than a large problem, she told herself.

She still didn't feel comfortable about it.

Margaret nodded. "You obviously had a lot to...talk about," her mother said, mimicking her cadence. They were walking toward the staircase and she was having trouble with her hip. Another new malady, she thought with a frustrated sigh. Always something. "Well, now that you're home, I can go to bed."

The declaration amused Claire as she took small steps, guiding her mother.

"How did you go to bed all those nights I wasn't here?" she asked. She'd always told her mother where she would be, in case she wanted to write. While she served in Africa, letters from home were treasured. How had her mother adjusted to her living in such dangerous conditions?

Margaret laughed, mostly at herself. "I spent a lot of nights falling asleep here on the sofa. It made me feel closer to you and your father. You both spent a lot of time there." She placed a supportive hand to the small of her back. "Could be why I have so much back pain," she theorized. Just as she got to the base of the stairs, Margaret stopped. One hand on the banister, she raised her head and looked at her daughter. "Is he good?" she asked.

Claire felt slightly lost. As Margaret began moving again, Claire matched her step for step. It wasn't easy. "Who?"

"Caleb, of course," Margaret said with a touch of impatience. "Is he good...at talking?"

Claire had no idea if her mother was just slightly muddled because she was still half-asleep, or if she saw right through the excuse.

For better or for worse, Claire decided to continue the game. "Yes, he is."

Margaret nodded, as if she expected as much. "Good to know."

They reached the top and her mother deliberately let go of her arm, wanting to go the rest of the distance on her own. She stayed close to one wall as she made her way to her room.

Claire watched her progress, not knowing what to make of the exchange they'd just had. Should she comment on it? Ask her mother if she thought that something was going on between her and Caleb?

No, for now, it would probably be best just to let it go. With any luck, her mother was just talking in circles and didn't mean anything by it. Most likely, guilt, that emotion she'd been missing initially, just made her read things into her mother's words. Her mother probably didn't mean it to sound the way that it had.

But Claire doubted it.

The huge butterflies in her stomach told Claire that she wasn't sure just how she was going to face Caleb the next time she saw him. For that matter, she had no idea how he was going to act, either.

Would he ignore her? Act like nothing had happened? Or just elect to drop out of sight?

Heaven knew she'd heard more than her share of stories about all of the above, men not wanting to bother with a woman once the goal was secured.

No, Caleb wasn't like that.

Was he?

When Saturday morning arrived, she spent half of her time listening for the sound of a car pulling up in her driveway. There'd been a few false starts, but no one came, not even by mistake. By the time noon rolled around, Claire figured she had her answer.

"So where is he?" Margaret queried, coming up behind her in the living room. Her mother nodded toward the bay window that looked out on the driveway, indicating that neither Caleb nor his truck were there. "Caleb isn't going to leave the house half-painted, is he?" she asked, a critical tone entering her voice.

"I'm sure something came up." Although, when she saw Danny in the school yard yesterday, lining up for the bus, he'd said something about seeing her today.

Still, something could have come up at the last minute, she silently argued. Caleb was a police detective and while his beat was vice, not homicide, his line of work wasn't exactly the kind you could use to set a schedule to, either.

"Oh, never mind," Margaret said in the next breath, waving away any explanation that Claire could have come up with. "They're here."

Her mother, Claire noted, lit up like a Christmas tree, even though she tried to pretend that she was indifferent to the people climbing out of the truck.

Yeah, right, Claire thought.

As for her, her stomach suddenly gave birth to quite possibly the largest butterfly ever to have materialized in the known western hemisphere.

Chapter Thirteen

It wasn't like him. For some reason, he was running behind today and now he couldn't find Danny. Where the hell had that boy gotten to? He wasn't in the house. Danny looked forward to these trips over to Claire's house even more than he did.

Well, maybe that wasn't quite right, but it soothed his conscience to think that right now, in light of what had happened last week.

Damn, but he felt conflicted. "Danny, where are you?" he called out impatiently. "We've got to get going."

This time, rather than silence, he heard his son answer, "Right here." The next moment, Danny came into the living room, a bunch of bedraggled, drooping daisies that had seen better days clutched in his hand.

Caleb stiffened when he saw the flowers. Jane had planted daisies in the backyard when they'd moved in.

"What are you doing with those?" Caleb asked.

"They're Mama's favorites," Danny said as if that was to answer everything.

"I know that," Caleb heard himself snapping. He struggled to regain control over a temper that was way too short today. "But what are you…?"

"Today's her birthday," Danny explained. He put the daisies beside the framed photograph of the three of them that was on the coffee table. The daisies spread out in front of the frame like leaves that had been scattered by the wind.

Jane's birthday. How could he have forgotten? There was a sudden heaviness in his chest. It only intensified as Danny raised his teary eyes up to him. "Think she can see them?"

Caleb sat down on the sofa and gathered the boy to him. "I know she can," he answered, his voice barely above a whisper. He knew that was what the boy needed to hear. As for himself, he hadn't a clue. There was an incredible sadness within him and it had breached all the barriers he'd held in place.

"I miss her, Dad," Danny sobbed. "I miss her lots."

He held the boy against him, feeling Danny's tears against his shoulder. Feeling his own tears welling up. "Me, too, Danny," Caleb said hoarsely. "Me, too."

His cell phone began to ring, but he ignored it. Comforting his son was far more important.

There was something different about Caleb when he got out of the car. She noticed it immediately. He seemed exceedingly uncomfortable.

She knew it.

In addition to the giant butterfly, she felt a sinking

sensation in her stomach. Things were not going to be the same again between her and Caleb. Ever. They'd crossed a line and now there was no going back.

She'd lost him as a friend and she sincerely mourned that.

Claire walked out the front door, leaving it open for her mother. Because she and Caleb weren't alone, she put on a smile and pretended that she didn't know that there was something wrong—or the reason behind it.

"My mother was beginning to think you weren't going to come today," she said pleasantly. The next moment, Danny reached her and threw his arms around her waist. Looking up, he gave her a huge smile and a sunny "Hi!" She ran her hand over the boy's already tousled hair.

She was really going to miss this, she thought, struggling to keep the sadness out of her eyes.

"Your mother's half-right," Caleb told her, hooking his thumbs in the corners of his pockets. He was obviously struggling to get his words out.

Releasing Danny, she let him run into the house and to her mother, who was waiting for him. She glanced over her shoulder to make sure that neither was in hearing range, then she approached Caleb.

"You don't have to feel obligated to come here, Caleb," she told him, lowering her voice even more. "You've done more around the house than I could ever begin to repay you for and, well…" How did she put this? "I just don't want you to feel awkward."

"Well, I do," he bit off. Then, as she searched for something appropriate to say, Caleb continued with the rest of it. "I don't like asking for favors."

In the blink of an eye, he'd completely lost her.

She'd assumed the awkward expression was due to the fallout after making love with her. But apparently something else was to blame. "What favor?"

"I've got to go in." The call that he hadn't answered immediately had been from the precinct. He needed to go in. Ordinarily, he would have called to tell her that he wasn't coming. But then his options fell through. "Can't go into details," he told her. "But Mrs. Collins made plans to visit her sister in Santa Barbara today and I need someone to watch Danny for me until I get back." He frowned. He hated imposing.

It took her a second to catch her breath. Relief flooded her. Claire stared at him, feeling oddly giddy and annoyed with herself at the same time for getting so carried away.

"Is that it?" she asked.

"No. I intend to pay you what I pay Mrs. Collins," he told her. If he paid Claire, then he was a little less in debt to her.

"You do and I'll make you eat it," she informed him calmly. "You've been working on the house every weekend for over a couple of months now. I can certainly do this for you. Besides, Danny's great company. I should be paying you." She looked at him, wanting to be sure. "And that's really it? There's no other reason you look like a ball player whose uniform is two sizes too small and strangling you?"

She came up with the strangest comparisons, he thought. "No, why? Should there be?"

Cut bait and run. Just say no. But part of her felt that she needed to have all this out now, while it was still fresh.

"I just thought...after last Sunday..."

How in heaven's name did she phrase this without

sounding like her every thought centered on their love-making? On her very first experience into that incredibly wondrous realm? Her every thought *hadn't* been centered on their lovemaking. It was her every *other* thought that had gone there.

And then suddenly, she couldn't say anything. Danny returned, his lively eyes bright with anticipation. "Miss Santaniello, can I play with the video set? Your mom said it was okay, but I thought I should check with you."

Lord, but he was well trained. He had better manners than most adults. She put her hand on his shoulder. "Sweetheart, you can play with anything you want." She'd purchased the new video console exclusively to entertain the boy. Who would have known that Danny would teach her mother how to play? "But go easy on my mother. Remember, she's just getting the hang of the game."

"Okay," he promised cheerfully, ducking back into the house. "Bye, Dad," he sang out just before he disappeared from view. In a second, the melodic theme song programmed into the video game came drifting out through the open window in the family room.

Caleb glanced at his watch. He didn't really have to see it to know he was running really late now. Even so, he remained where he was for a moment longer. She'd said something and it needed to be cleared up. Ordinarily, he would have just ignored the subject. But this was Claire and she deserved better treatment at his hands.

"Did you think I just wasn't going to show up today, after being here every single Saturday and most Sundays for more than the last two months, because of…what happened between us?"

Caleb hadn't called it sex, she thought, grateful for the small crumb. She was fairly certain he probably didn't think of what had happened as love-making, but at least it wasn't just plain sex to him. And who knew, maybe it was just the slightest bit special to him, too.

"I wasn't sure what to think," she admitted quietly. "I don't exactly have firsthand experience in this sort of thing. And etiquette books don't cover the proper way people who aren't married behave toward one another...afterward." Before she could continue to verbally stumble about, a low hum, like the sound of an electric toothbrush, broke through. *Saved!* She nodded toward the phone clipped to his belt. "I think someone's trying to reach you."

Caleb suppressed an exasperated sigh. More than likely, it was Ski, calling to find out where the hell he was. He planned to be on his way in less than five minutes. For a second, he debated taking the easy way out, then decided against it. As much as he didn't like talking about personal matters, this did need to be addressed, otherwise he couldn't put it out of the way.

"He can wait." Caleb ignored the vibrating phone. "Look, I don't exactly know what's going on," he confessed. "But I think that maybe you should know that I haven't been with a woman since Jane died. The thought of being with another woman hadn't even crossed my mind. Jane was very, very special to me."

Now he was coming off like some plaster saint and that definitely wasn't what he was trying to convey. He tried again.

"Don't get me wrong, we had our differences and our arguments. Some of them got pretty vocal," he recalled. "Especially about her work. But I felt things for Jane, things that I can't even begin to put into words."

Dead or not, she envied Jane. Envied her for finding a love that rich, that overwhelming. She nodded. "I understand."

"No," he told her, "I don't think you do. I felt things for her that I knew I'd never feel again. And I didn't. I didn't feel anything at all after she was killed—except lost and angry. I was pretty resigned that was the way things were going to be from then on. And then you came back. And, hell, I don't know…" He threw up his hands as his voice trailed off.

Just when she thought he was going to walk away from her and get into his truck, leaving his sentence just hanging, unfinished, in the air, Caleb surprised her by resorting to another method to show her what he was trying to say.

Grabbing her by the arms, he pulled her to him and sealed his mouth to hers. Hard.

The kiss was quick, but far from fleeting. Because in that one instant, he penetrated her very core, leaving her shaken, dizzy and so wanting more.

Pulling back, Caleb opened his hands and released his hold on her. His expression indicated how frustrated he was.

"I can't put it any better than that," he told her tersely. And then the next moment, he was striding toward his car.

She came to just as he lowered himself into the cab of his car. Claire ran over to the vehicle. "When will you be back?" She was breathless, but running had absolutely nothing to do with it.

He shrugged carelessly. "I don't know. Sometime today. It's the best I can do." And then he realized why she was asking. Or thought he did. "Did you have plans for later today?"

She shook her head, determined not to let him see that she was more confused than ever by his explanation. But she supposed it was all right. She didn't know how she felt about everything, either. Except that she didn't want to lose him as a friend.

"I just want to know if Danny is staying for dinner."

Caleb nodded as he started up the car.

The rattle of the engine kicking in mimicked her emotions as the sound seemed to bounce all over the place. It seemed to her that the longer she was away from the order, the more confused she felt. Wasn't it supposed to be the other way around?

"Stay safe," Claire called to him just before he pulled away.

His response was almost inaudible. It took her a few seconds to play it back in her head and make sense of it. He'd muttered, "I'll do my best," just before he was out of earshot.

"So will I, Caleb," she murmured. "So will I." Whatever her best was, she added silently, because right now, she hadn't a clue. She was flying without a compass with guilt and confusion as her copilots.

Caleb didn't return until a little more than an hour into the next day. One-ten in the morning. Tired but too keyed up to sleep, Claire had waited up for him. Listening for the approach of his car, she was on her feet before he had a chance to shut off the engine.

She rushed to the front door and opened it just as

he came up the front walk. Her greeting never had a chance to emerge.

He scowled at her as he came in. "Don't you know better than to fling open your door like that this time of night?" He bit the words off one by one like well-aimed bullets. He'd seen too many things happen to take safety for granted.

"Nope," she said cheerfully. "Besides, my friend, the vice cop, was due here any minute." Claire closed the door behind him. "I figured I was safe." Coming around, she took a closer look at his face and her bantering tone faded. "You look exhausted. Didn't it go well?" She knew she couldn't ask specific questions, but this one seemed nebulous enough to merit an answer.

"Yeah. Finally."

He'd had to chase down one of the so-called "suspects" over an obstacle course that would have gladdened the hearts of an entire Olympic marathon committee before he'd managed to tackle the man and bring him down. He knew he was going to pay for both the sprint and the tackle come morning. While he worked out with weights whenever he could, running had never been his thing. Right about now, especially after having come down so hard on the pavement, he felt like something the cat wouldn't have dragged in on a bet.

Taking a deep breath, he scanned the living room. "Where's Danny?"

Claire nodded toward the stairs. "Asleep in the guest room. I put him down at nine and read to him for almost an hour." She smiled, remembering. "He tried very hard to stay awake for you, but eventually, he lost the struggle."

He nodded. Just as well. He felt too tired to talk to the boy and he didn't want Danny to misunderstand. They'd covered a lot of ground this morning, even without words. He didn't want anything jeopardizing that.

Caleb turned toward the stairs. "I'll just go get him and be on my way."

Claire shifted so that she blocked his way. "Why don't you let him sleep. He's fine where he is. I certainly don't mind having him here." Caleb looked as if he was barely awake himself. "You look like you're dead on your feet. You're welcome to stay here, too. I can make up the sofa for you."

Caleb rotated his shoulders. The ache was already beginning to set in. He was grateful to her for keeping his son overnight. It simplified his exit. He could just flop on the couch at home.

"No, thanks." He turned back toward the front door. "I'll just go to the house."

She noticed that he didn't refer to it as home. Was that because he didn't think of it as home anymore now that his wife was gone? Her heart ached for him.

Very gently, she took his hand and steered him toward the sofa. "Why don't you sit down for a minute," she coaxed. "In your present condition you're liable to fall asleep behind the wheel. I *really* don't want to have that on my conscience."

The word *no* was right there but somehow, it didn't come out. Before he knew it, he found himself sitting on the sofa. The cushions seductively molded themselves around him. He sighed. "You really know how to wield that guilt thing, don't you?"

Claire laughed. "Hey, I'm Italian and Catholic, guilt

is part of my makeup," she quipped. "Now stay down," she instructed when he looked as if he was going to get up—or try to. To make sure her message got across, she kept her hand on his shoulder for a moment for good measure. "I'll get you something to drink," she offered. "Orange juice okay?"

"Fine," he murmured. She lifted her hand carefully, watching him. Satisfied that he wasn't going anywhere, she turned on her heel and began to cross to the kitchen. "Claire?"

Stopping, she glanced at him over her shoulder. "Yes?"

"If something happens to me, I'd like you to look after Danny."

She'd expected him to say something about changing his mind about the orange juice and asking for something else. This came flying at her like a winged monkey out of an abyss. Stunned, thinking that maybe she'd misheard, she crossed back to him.

"What?"

Maybe he should have worded it better. Communication was not his long suit. Neither was timing, he supposed. But this had been preying on his mind since late this afternoon. He wasn't about to get any peace until he settled the matter.

"Look." He sat up. "I know it's a big favor and I wouldn't ask, but there is no one else." That almost sounded insulting, he realized and tried again to explain. "Jane was an only child, like me, and her parents are dead, also like me." Her father had died less than two months after she did. "If something happens to me, I don't want Danny getting lost in the system."

He supposed he could ask his partner to look after

Danny, but all things considered, Claire was far better equipped to raise his son. And if he asked Ski, the man would take the request to mean that they'd become closer and start asking all sorts of questions. Ski read something positive into almost anything. Getting Claire to say yes was better for everyone all around.

Claire gazed down at him and tried to read between the lines. The orange juice could wait. She sat down beside him on the sofa, her eyes never leaving his. "What happened tonight?"

"Nothing," he retorted. "I just had some time to think, that's all."

He'd said *nothing* much too fast, she thought. She began to understand why he said so little. It was because he didn't lie very well. She studied his face for a long moment.

"What?" he snapped.

"You do know that it's a sin to lie to a sister of the Dominican order, don't you?"

His eyes narrowed. Was she having second thoughts about her decision? Had making love caused her to want to return to the shelter of her previous life?

"I thought you said—"

"Even an ex-sister of the Dominican order," she amended. And then she became serious again. "What happened tonight?"

In general, tonight had been a huge success. They'd broken up a kiddy porn studio tonight. But he'd taken a bullet to the chest when they stormed the floating studio. If he hadn't been wearing his bulletproof vest, or if the shooter's aim had been a bit higher, he wouldn't have made it back tonight.

As it was, the impact of the shot had knocked him

off his feet, dazing him. Ever since Jane's death, he'd been wishing for oblivion, praying for death. But now that it had almost happened, the first thing on his mind had been Danny. From what he had heard and seen, from everything that Jane had told him, there was nothing worse for a child than to be passed around within the foster system. He couldn't do that to Danny. But not everything was within his control. Which was where Claire came in.

He looked at her. She was still waiting for an answer. Knowing that Claire wasn't about to back off without something, he shrugged, trying to make the incident insignificant. "There was a raid tonight and there was gunfire—"

The moment he said it, her eyes lowered, looking for a sign that he'd been hit. When she didn't see anything immediately, she pulled apart his jacket to make sure he wasn't hiding something.

That was when she saw the hole in his shirt.

"Whoa." Pulling back, he stilled her hands. "I didn't get hit."

"Then what's that?" she demanded, nodding toward the hole in his shirt.

He looked down even though he knew what she was referring to. "That's where the bullet met my vest," he told her matter-of-factly.

Claire's eyes widened. Her thoughts began to scramble and she had to grasp on to them to keep them from flying in directions she didn't want to go. "Oh God. Are you sure you're all right?"

"I'm fine," he assured her gruffly, although her concern did touch him. More than he was comfortable about admitting. "It just knocked the wind out of me—

and started me thinking about Danny." He looked at her. "You haven't given me an answer."

Did he really think he needed one? "That's because it goes without saying. Of course I'll look after him. Just have the papers drawn up, I'll sign them. And hope we never need them," she added with feeling. Claire rose to her feet again. "Now wait right here and let me get that juice."

Caleb leaned back against the sofa again. "Yes, ma'am."

She smiled to herself as she left the room. It took her exactly two minutes to get the juice, pour it into a glass and return with it.

The same amount of time it took Caleb to fall asleep.

Looking at him, her smile widened. He was staying the night after all.

Claire set down the glass on the coffee table, in case he woke up and wanted it. Seeing him like this, she thought he almost looked peaceful.

About time.

She covered him with the throw that hung over the back of the sofa and quietly backed away.

Chapter Fourteen

"What are you doing about Thanksgiving?"

Crouching beneath the master bathroom sink like an early Christian martyr doing penance, Caleb had thought he was alone. The sound of Claire's voice caught him off guard and had him smashing the top of his head against some very unforgiving porcelain.

He swallowed a curse—just barely—and crawled away from the pipes he was still reattaching to the brand-new sink he'd installed earlier. Sitting on the ice-blue tile—installed last week—he looked up at her. His expression at the moment was far from friendly.

Caleb rubbed the top of his head. Tiny devils with tinier anvils shot through his system. It was all he could do not to wince. "I'm letting it happen, same as I do every year."

Claire shook her head and crouched down beside

him. She preferred being eye to eye with Caleb when she was trying to convince him of something.

"No, I mean do you have any plans?" He was still looking at her as if she had suddenly lapsed into some foreign language he couldn't begin to place. *Once more with feeling.* "Are you and Danny invited any-where?" she enunciated slowly.

As a matter of fact, Ski had extended an invitation just the other day, but he refused to take his partner up on it. The man was already way too chummy. He didn't need to get to know the man's wife and two kids any better than he already knew them.

"No."

She thought as much. She had no idea just where this relationship of theirs was going to go, but she didn't want either him or his son spending the holidays isolated. "Well, you are now."

Knowing where this was going—and what the probable outcome was going to be, he was still going to make her work for it. He didn't want her feeling too confident. This despite the fact that they, he, Danny and Claire, were spending more and more time together. They'd gone to Knott's Berry Farm just the other weekend, finally using the tickets that Mrs. Collins had given him plus buying two more because Claire's mother had come with them. Danny had insisted on pushing the wheelchair that Margaret had been forced to use in order not to become too tired. Everyone had had a good time, even him.

They were becoming a unit. The thought would have worried him if he allowed himself to dwell on it. But every time his thoughts became introspective, he shut them down. To dwell on them would have made him instinctively pull back. Because he'd anticipate pain at the end of the road. It was a given.

"Where?" he deadpanned.

"Here," she answered. "It'd be good for Danny, good for my mother." She actually needed this as much as Caleb did, she thought. "She's not doing too well again," she confided. She'd seen it coming for a while now. The lab workup at their last visit confirmed it. The short-lived remission was officially over. The leukemia had returned and was aggressive. "Having Danny around helps her forget about things."

Caleb studied her for a moment, trying to ignore the fact that being this close to her aroused feelings he still tried to keep under lock and key. He wasn't successful. She looked so hopeful, so enthusiastic, he was finding her increasingly difficult to resist.

"So this counts as a good deed if I say yes?"

Her head bobbed up and down vigorously, her silky red hair brushing against his bare arm. "Definitely."

For a second, he struggled against the urge to pull her into his arms. But her mother or Danny could walk in at any moment and he wasn't ready to let anyone else know that his feelings were not as removed as he wanted them to be.

His eyes searched her face for some sort of indication. "What about you?"

She wasn't sure she understood what he was asking. Maybe she was too caught up in watching his mouth, she thought, upbraiding herself. "What about me what?"

He rose to his feet, dusting off his hands on the back of his jeans, then gave her a hand up, as well. She came up a little too fast and a little too close. Crowding his space. Crowding him. He didn't mind nearly as much as he should have.

Belatedly, he remembered to let go of her hand. "You said having us over would be good for Danny and your mother. What about you? Would it be good for you?"

The very words brushed along her skin, waking up every single pulse point on her body. Her eyes held his and she heard herself saying, "That goes without saying."

He surprised her by running his finger down her nose. It was a playful gesture that was completely out of character for the adult Caleb. But not for the boy she had once known.

"Nothing goes without saying," he told her. With that, he turned away, feeling much too compromised at the moment. He began rummaging through the toolbox on the counter. He needed to get back to work if this sink was going to be functioning by the time he left.

She found herself addressing his back. "That is a very odd philosophy for a man who could give the Sphinx a run for its money."

He glanced up at the mirror, their eyes meeting briefly via their reflections. "The Sphinx doesn't run."

Claire laughed, shaking her head. "Are you baiting me?"

The shoulders beneath the faded denim shirt rose and then fell in a careless movement. "Maybe, just a little. I have so few hobbies."

This was the old Caleb, she thought happily, the one she remembered so fondly. The one who had a sense of humor about himself. "Protecting and serving and being the world's best handyman isn't enough for you?"

Finding the tool he needed, he closed the box. "I'm hardly the best." He snorted.

Taking hold of him by the shoulders, she deliberately turned him around to face her. "You show up like clockwork. You refuse to let me pay you and you complete every job you start. *And* you take on jobs that you don't have to." She paused for a second. "If that's not the best, then I don't know what is."

A smile played on her lips, but it was fairly obvious to him that Claire no longer was talking just about his being a handyman.

His eyes met hers. "Maybe it's because you haven't had any experience...in handymen," he added significantly.

"Some things," she said as she felt a blush creeping up along her neck, feeding up onto her cheeks, "you just know. I don't need to take an extensive survey—a survey of any kind, actually—to prove that I'm right. It's a given." She didn't need experience to know that he was a patient, giving lover. If the experience hadn't been as wonderful as it was, the guilt of having wantonly made love would have eaten away at her until there would have been nothing left. As it was, she had to struggle not to let guilt take possession of her in the wee hours of the night, when the world was blackest and all things bad were magnified.

So much for working, Caleb thought, placing the tool back down on top of the toolbox. He glanced toward the doorway to make sure that neither Danny nor her mother were there. He didn't want to be overheard. This was far too personal.

Taking hold of her arms, Caleb looked at her for a long moment. Who would have ever thought…?

"You know, you've been on my mind ever since…"

She nodded. He was struggling to put this into words and she didn't want him to feel as if he was on the spot. "Yes, me, too."

"I'd like to take you out again. Just the two of us," he emphasized in case she misunderstood. Hell, he would have liked to take her right here, on the tile floor he'd installed. Only an exceeding amount of restraint kept him from acting on his impulse. "And then bring you home again," he added so that his meaning was clear. "I find myself thinking about you when I shouldn't be."

He found it harder and harder to keep his mind on his work *while* at work. That had never happened to him before. He had an iron will and could channel his thoughts as needed. His ability to concentrate, to focus on only one thing, was exceptional.

Until now.

Lately, thoughts of Claire would break in, like interference on an out-of-area radio station. Damn, but she had scrambled his head. If he knew what was good for him, he'd grab his son and head for the hills.

But he didn't know what was good for him. He just wanted her. "I want to make love with you again," he told her, his voice low but no less intense for the lack of volume.

Her mouth curved. Everything he'd just said went twice for her. She stood just inside the threshold of a brand-new, brave world, stripped of her common sense and incredibly eager to go forward. What would the other sisters have said if they could have seen her now?

They probably would have all fervently prayed for her soul—while she prayed for something else.

She was blaspheming—so why did she feel like smiling? No one had warned her that being in the secular world would be so complicated.

"You've been sent here to tempt me, haven't you?"

"If anything," he theorized, "it's the other way around. How about tomorrow evening?" he pressed. Tomorrow was Sunday, low-key and unhurried in comparison to a Friday or Saturday night. It seemed like a perfect time to go out.

To his surprise, she shook her head. "Monday's Halloween."

He didn't see the connection. "Are you planning to turn into a bat at midnight?" he asked.

"No, I meant that I've got things to prepare. My class—"

"Claire, are you afraid of me?"

"I told you once. It's not you I'm afraid of. It's me." Because he was coming to mean so much to her. Both him and his son and despite all the obstacles she tried to set up.

"That makes sense. You're the scariest person I know," he deadpanned. When she looked at him, he grew serious. "Because you make me feel things again, things I swore to myself I'd never feel. Things, God help me, I *want* to feel." Even as he resisted, he thought. Caleb took her hand. "None of this has been easy for me, either. But you've made me realize that if you don't risk things, you're not alive."

He was giving her way too much credit. He'd done all the hard work. She was just there to pick up the slack once in a while. "I made you realize that, huh?"

He was deadly serious. "Yes."

She ran her hand along his cheek and felt a slight ripple travel through her palm and up her arm. "I guess I'm better than I thought."

He took her into his arms. "You have no idea."

Before she could say anything, he was kissing her again. Kissing her and making everything swirl around her, just like before. Except that her reaction happened far more quickly. Because she knew what was out there, what was waiting for her if she only let herself be swept away. There was no doubt about it, Caleb had the most incredible effect on her.

"Tomorrow," she murmured when he drew back again, an eternity later.

"Tomorrow?"

"I'll go out with you tomorrow. You asked, remember?" she reminded him. Taking a step back, she blew out a long breath, trying to get her bearings. "I'd better go start dinner. You're invited, by the way. You and Danny. But then, you already know that."

"Yes," he said under his breath, watching her leave the room, enjoying the way her jeans hugged her hips as she moved. He was going to have to get a grip, he told himself. But not yet. Not yet. "I already know that."

As she wove her way slowly up and down the aisles, proctoring the math exam her students were taking, Claire couldn't keep her thoughts from drifting beyond the classroom's gaily, holiday-decorated four walls. A great deal had happened in such a small space of time.

On the home front, Thanksgiving had turned out to be a huge success, despite the fact that the turkey required an extra hour in the oven. On a whim, she'd invited her cousin Nancy, Nancy's husband Patrick and their four kids to the dinner.

When he'd realized that there was going to be more people at the table than just the four of them, Caleb tried to beg off. But she succeeded in twisting his arm, pointing out how mingling with new people was good for Danny. She'd also taken him aside for a moment as he wavered and added that this was important to her. She didn't know how many more Thanksgivings her mother would be able to have.

It was a cold, hard truth, something she didn't like to think about, but she was not above using it to gain what she felt was best for everyone's sake. Faced with that, Caleb reluctantly changed his mind. Part of her knew that no one could make the vice detective do what he didn't want to do. Since he'd agreed, it meant that at least part of him wanted to be there.

It was progress. Tiny steps perhaps, but progress.

In more ways than one.

Since their initial night of lovemaking, she'd been with Caleb three more times and each time had turned out to be better than the last. They kept improving on perfection. But it hadn't been without cost. Because of all her religious training, there had been remorse, regret and surging stings of guilt that marred the euphoria. She did her best to hide those feelings but she knew that Caleb picked up on them. And just perhaps, they had added fuel to the struggle she knew in her heart he had to be going through himself.

They were on a rocky road, but she was determined not to let her fears keep her from moving forward. Because the rewards were so precious.

They were a little more than two weeks away from Christmas and there were a naked Christmas tree standing in the middle of the family room, waiting to be adorned. The four of them—she'd insisted that her mother come along and at least watch from the car—had selected a real tree from one of the nearby lots last night. To her surprise, Caleb, of his own volition, had brought each viable candidate over to the car for her mother to cast her vote for or against. Danny had excitedly brought up the rear while a none-too-happy lot owner suspiciously watched.

It had turned out to be a great bonding experience for father and son. In the end, her mother had picked out the tree that was in their family room—after consulting with Danny.

Looking over the sea of bent heads, Claire couldn't remember when she'd been happier.

Lost in thought, she didn't hear it at first. Not until it became louder and several of the children looked up and toward the door.

"Someone's knocking, Miss Santaniello." Jenny Altman, sitting in the first seat, first row, pointed toward the door.

The next moment, the principal's secretary, Shirley, opened the door and beckoned to her. "There's a call for you in the office, Claire."

Claire glanced over her shoulder. Ordinarily, if she stepped out, she'd leave one of the students in charge of the class. But they were all still busy taking the exam. "Take a message, Shirley," she requested. "I'll call whoever it is back right after my class is finished with their exam."

But Shirley looked a little hesitant. "She said it was urgent."

Something instantly tightened in her stomach. Urgent. She'd never liked that word, Claire thought. "Who?"

"Your cousin." Shirley paused, thinking. "Nancy I believe she said her name was."

The knot grew tighter. If she didn't take this call, her imagination was going to run away with her before she ever returned it. "Shirley, could you watch them for me? They're almost done."

Assuming the secretary's answer would be in the affirmative, Claire left before the woman had a chance to respond.

The hallway leading from her classroom to the main office felt longer than usual. It was hard to keep from running.

She was working herself up for no reason, Claire silently lectured. She knew Nancy's "urgent" calls. It was probably to ask about a recipe or to find out when they were all getting together again and at whose house. Normal things. No reason to feel as if her heart had lodged itself in her throat. Her mother had looked better this morning when she'd left than she had in the last week. This was probably nothing.

Claire still made it to the office in record time. Someone called out a "hello" and she barely acknowledged it. She couldn't have even said who it was. Heading straight for Shirley's desk, she picked up the receiver and released the hold button.

"Hello?" The word sounded shaky. There was a huge lump in her throat.

"Claire?" the voice on the other end asked.

Please, please, please ask me about a recipe, Nancy. Her hands felt damp as she held the receiver with both hands. "Yes?"

"Thank God." Nancy sounded breathless. "Claire, I've been trying to reach you on your cell phone, but it kept going to voice mail."

"I shut my phone off when I'm in the classroom." She was having an inane conversation while trying not to throw up. "What's the matter? What's wrong?" But even as she asked, Claire had a sinking sensation. Despite what she was trying to convince herself of, she knew that Nancy wouldn't have gone through the principal's office just to ask about something trivial. "It's Mother, isn't it?" She thought she heard Nancy stifle a sob before answering.

"Aunt Margaret called me a little while ago. I got to your house as quickly as I could." She drew in a ragged breath. "The ambulance just took her away."

Claire's hands went icy. "Ambulance? What ambulance?"

"The one I called. Oh, Claire, Aunt Margaret could hardly move. She didn't even seem like the person I saw yesterday. I thought she was dead when I got here." There was another sob and it was obvious that Nancy struggled to regain control. "She told me that it took her half an hour to get to the phone to call me."

The room was tilting. She could see Mr. Selkirk, one of the counselors, watching her as if she was going to faint. Claire turned away so he couldn't see her expression.

"But she was all right this morning," Claire insisted, as if that would change something. "Not great, but all right."

Her mother had been a little pale, perhaps, but she'd attributed that to her mother being up later than normal because of the Christmas tree excursion. Tears sprang to her eyes, blurring her vision. She angrily wiped them away with the back of her hand. She couldn't break down now, she had to be strong. There was no one to turn to.

"I'll be right there."

"Claire, I'm at home," Nancy told her quickly, afraid that Claire would break the connection before she knew. "Ethan's sick," she said, mentioning her youngest, "and I couldn't leave him for long. Call me as soon as you know anything."

"Okay." Shaking inside, Claire hung up. The moment she did, she dashed out into the hallway and ran back to her room.

"No running in the halls, Miss Santaniello," a tiny voice, belonging to a hall monitor, piped up.

Ordinarily, she would have stopped. But not this time. The sense of urgency refused to abate.

Shirley seemed relieved to see her. But then, the next moment, uncertainty entered the dark brown eyes.

"I've got to leave," Claire told her, taking her purse out of the bottom drawer where she kept it. "It's an emergency. They've just taken my mother to the hospital. Please tell Principal Walcott I'm very sorry."

"Is she all right, Miss Santaniello?" one of the little girls in the back of the room asked.

"Is your mom going to die?" another chimed in bluntly.

Trust a child to voice the thought she couldn't bring herself to entertain.

"I really hope not, Kyle," she tossed back as she made her exit.

* * *

Claire prayed all the way to the hospital. It had been a while since she'd prayed with this intense feeling of urgency. In the past, praying had always made her feel better. It didn't this time. She couldn't shake the feeling of dread.

"I know I can't tell You what to do and I have no right to ask. A lot of people think I walked out on You. But You know better, don't You? You understand that it just wasn't working out and that I could do better for both of us out here in the secular world than where I was.

"Or at least, I thought I could. But it's gotten all mixed up, hasn't it?" Her head was hurting. She had trouble keeping her eyes on the road. "Are You doing this to punish me for sleeping with Caleb? If I stop, will she be all right?"

She was babbling now and she knew it, but she was trying her best to collect herself. She needed to be calm when she went to see her mother. Her mother would take her cue from her.

"Please, don't take her away." Her voice cracked. She swallowed, trying to get rid of the dusty sensation in her throat. "Not yet. Let me have her for a little while longer. We're just getting to know each other again after all these years. I gave those years to You. Couldn't You please give me a few more months with her?" She blinked several times to clear the haze from her eyes again. Approaching the hospital parking lot, she made her way to the first lot she could find.

"I don't mean to sound as if I'm making demands," she murmured. "But if You could find it in Your heart to spare her for a while, I would really take it as a personal favor."

When she'd been younger, before she ever entered the order, she would make deals with God, offering to give up something if only she could have what she was praying for. She desperately wanted to do that again, but she had nothing to offer anymore.

Nothing except one thing.

Claire took a deep breath. "If You spare her, if You let my mother live, I'll go back to the order. If she goes into remission, I'll take it as a sign that I made a mistake and that You want me to go back. All right?"

Her words echoed back to her. She felt empty inside. Empty and scared.

"I'll assume You said yes."

Fighting back tears, Claire hurried to the back entrance of the hospital's emergency room.

Chapter Fifteen

Claire thought she was braced when she entered her mother's small room on the fifth floor.

She was wrong.

Never a large woman, Margaret Santaniello looked positively tiny and oh-so-lost against the white sheets of the hospital bed.

Tubes and wires ran up and down the length of her frail body, monitoring functions, deadening her pain, helping her breathe and warding off any stray infections.

A wave of weakness washed over Claire and she held on to the doorknob for a moment to steady herself, afraid that she was going to collapse.

It wasn't that she'd never seen frail, sick people before. She had. On almost a regular basis. Women old before their time, before they'd even reached their twenties; skinny, malnourished babies with distended bellies; scrawny, skeletonlike men who were taken down by the ravages of diseases before they'd even had a chance to live.

But this was different.

This twisted her heart so that she could hardly stand it.

This was her mother.

She supposed, in a way, she'd expected her mother to live forever, to continue, as she had always done. Even when she hadn't been able to see her mother for long spans of time, in the back of her mind, her mother was always there. *Would* always be there.

Except now, she might not be.

Claire couldn't bring herself to remove the words *might not* and substitute *wouldn't*. She wasn't strong enough for that yet.

Her knees solidified, she took a deep breath and slowly approached the narrow hospital bed, taking care not to bump against any of the machines that seemed to have taken up most of the available space.

Her mother opened her eyes. "You…came." The two-word sentence was uttered breathlessly, as if it took a great deal of strength and will just to make it materialize.

How could her mother have expected anything else? "Of course I came. The second that Nancy called me." She picked up her mother's hand and laced her fingers through her mother's. They felt cold, Claire thought, struggling against a huge wave of despair that threatened to engulf her. "Why wouldn't I?"

Margaret struggled to smile. It was an effort only half-completed. Each word emerged after a breathless pause. "No, I knew...you'd come.... I just didn't know...if...I...would still be...here."

"Don't talk like that," Claire cried. She lowered her tone. "Mother, you've got to stop this negative attitude. It's weighing you down. You're not going anywhere," Claire told her fiercely. She realized that she'd tightened her hold on her mother's hand and loosened her grip. She needed to restrain the mounting panic she felt. "You're going to stay here for a little while," she said in a softer voice, "get better and then I'll take you home."

This time, her mother managed to curve her lips in a small smile. "I'm not...leaving here and we both...know that."

"No, we don't," Claire insisted. "No, we don't," she repeated with more feeling.

"And when...I go...home," her mother continued, as if she hadn't said anything, "it won't be to...the house on...Hamilton...Street. It'll be home...to...God and your...father." Her breathing grew more and more labored.

Claire held on to her mother's hand harder, as if the very act would anchor her mother's spirit to the bed. To her.

"Dad's just going to have to wait a while longer. Don't rush things, Mother." She was blinking hard now, trying to keep the tears from flowing. They fell anyway. "Christmas is coming. How am I going to be able to decorate the tree if you're not there, telling me where to hang everything?"

"I never...did...that."

"Yes, you did," Claire reminded her fondly. "And it drove me crazy at the time, but I promise..." Tears were choking her. "I promise it won't this time."

Margaret paused, gathering her strength and her breath. There was one more thing she needed to say. "You can go back now," she told her daughter.

Was she sending her away? Claire didn't understand. "Go back?"

"To the order. Once...I'm gone...you won't need...to stay. You...can...go...back." Margaret's eyes looked cloudy as they searched for her face. Her voice was hardly a whisper now. "You will go back... won't...you?"

Claire didn't want to waste her mother's breath talking about that. She wanted her to save her strength. "We'll talk about it once you're home."

Margaret appeared to grow agitated. She moved her head from side to side. "Claire, it was all I...could do to hang...on...until you got here. I'm...tired, but I...want to go...without you on...my...conscience. Tell me...you'll go back."

This was important to her mother. And this wasn't the time to argue. "I'll go back."

"Good." Margaret's eyes began to drift shut, her face growing peaceful. "I love you. It'll...be nice...to see...your...father...again. I don't know...what he's been...doing all these...years without...me."

"Waiting," Claire told her quietly. The lump in her throat grew and she all but choked on her tears.

And then she felt the hand that was in hers go lax.

Panic and sorrow overwhelmed her. "Mother? Mom? Mom! Please don't go. *Please.*"

But even as she begged, she knew she was only talking to the shell that had once contained the spirit that had been her mother.

Margaret Santaniello was gone.

And she was alone.

This time, Claire didn't bother trying to control the tears that flooded her eyes. Sobbing, she put her arms around the frail body lying in the hospital bed and embraced her mother one last time.

There would be no team of doctors and nurses bursting through the door, pushing a crash cart before them, utilizing heroic methods to try to bring Margaret Santaniello back from the dead. Her mother had told her that she had a DNR in place. A document that ordered the hospital staff: do not resuscitate. More than anything, Claire wanted to rescind it, wanted that team in here, fighting to save her mother. But she knew that would be imposing her will on her mother and she hadn't the right.

This was what her mother wanted. To be let go when the time came.

But she wasn't ready. And it would be oh, so terrible without her mother.

She heard the door behind her being opened. Probably someone from the nurses' station coming in to check if her mother was indeed gone.

Claire couldn't even raise her head to look. She couldn't stop crying. It was as if once she'd begun, that was all there was. Just tears and sorrow.

She couldn't even draw in a full breath.

And then, through a haze of pain and heartbreak, Claire felt strong arms lift her up from the bed and then turn her around. Felt a strong chest give her a place to bury her face and go on sobbing.

She did, for several long minutes. And then, drawing in a deep, ragged breath, she raised her head and found herself looking up at Caleb.

Was she hallucinating?

"What are you doing here?" She could hardly talk. Her throat was completely raw.

"Your cousin, Nancy, called the dispatch officer and dispatch got in contact with me."

He and Ski were checking out rumors of yet another underage pornography ring in the area, this one said to also pimp out their "starlets." They'd been in the middle of posing as two pedophiles, something they both found particularly vile, when he'd gotten the call from dispatch. He'd thought something had happened to Danny again until he heard Nancy's voice.

"She said she thought that you were going to need me. I left Ski holding the fort." His partner had been far from happy, but the man had rallied when Ski realized that he was coming to the aid of a woman. He'd left his partner bursting at the seams with unanswered questions. "I came as soon as I could."

He looked over Claire's head at Margaret. It was wrong what they said. People didn't look like they were asleep when they died. They just looked as if they'd died, as if some unknown "something"—a soul?—had disappeared, leaving them behind.

His arms tightened protectively around Claire. "I'm sorry, Claire. She was a really nice woman."

Claire tried to answer him, to say something, anything, in return. But the words wouldn't come. The tears wouldn't let them. All she could do was cry her heart out.

Very gently, Caleb pushed her head back down against his chest and let her cry. He held her to him until she finished.

He held her for a very long time.

Caleb waited in the wings while she made all the

arrangements she could at the hospital. Waited as she called her cousin to tell her what had happened. When her voice broke and she couldn't go on, he took the phone from her and told Nancy the rest of it.

Hanging up, he said, "You're coming home with me."

She shook her head. "No, that's all right, thank you."

"You don't understand," he told her, taking her arm. "This isn't negotiable. You're coming home with me. I don't want you to be alone."

"My car—" she began to protest.

He wasn't about to get sidetracked. "I'll have someone from the squad get it and bring it to your house. Any other arguments?"

She shook her head. "No."

"Good." Letting go of her arm, he slipped his arm protectively around her shoulders, gently but firmly guiding her out.

When Danny came home from school, he seemed surprised to find both his father and the woman he considered his best friend at home instead of Mrs. Collins.

The boy was about to call out a greeting to her and launch himself around her waist as was his custom away from school when he abruptly stopped.

Cocking his head, he looked at her more closely. "You look sad, Miss Santaniello."

"Her mother died today," Caleb told his son frankly. He expected the boy to back away.

Instead, Danny came closer and took Claire's hand. "It's okay, Miss Santaniello. She's with my mom. Mom'll take care of her."

Up until that moment, she was succeeding in her effort to put on a brave face in front of Caleb's son. But that bit of simple, tender philosophy, rendered by an eight-year-old, completely undid her. Fresh tears welled up in her eyes. She didn't bother to wipe them away as they slid down her cheeks.

When he seemed upset at her reaction, she did her best to smile at him. "Thank you, Danny. I think my mother would like that."

"Would you like something to eat?" Caleb asked his son.

"Mrs. Collins usually has a snack for me," Danny volunteered.

Caleb looked at Claire. "Why don't we see what we can do about that," he suggested. His goal was to keep her moving, to keep her busy. Staying busy was the only temporary solution he knew to the sort of pain she was dealing with.

She nodded, putting her hand on the boy's shoulders and leading the way to the kitchen. She drew in a ragged breath. "Sounds like a plan to me."

He didn't ask Claire until after Danny had gone to bed and she had turned down his offer to give her something that would help her sleep. He'd already made up his mind to keep her company until such time as she fell asleep on her own. And if she remained up all night, well, that was no big deal, either. It wouldn't be any different for him than all those nights that he'd been forced to put in on a stakeout.

They were standing outside on his porch, gazing up at a sky that was utterly devoid of any lights. The stars were conspicuously absent and the moon was new.

The only illumination came from the streetlamp and the lights from the other houses on the block.

The question had been burning in his brain ever since he'd overheard her final conversation with her mother. Now that they were alone, he had to ask. "So when are you going back?"

Claire looked at him, surprised by the blunt question. She shrugged. "I can go now if you'd like."

Why would she assume that he wanted to see her return to the order? Didn't she realize by now how he felt about her? What she had come to mean to him and to his son? Okay, maybe he'd been a little standoffish from time to time but that was only because he was trying to sort things out, to unshackle himself from both fear and guilt. After all, he hadn't expected to ever feel anything for another woman.

Maybe her mother's death had muddled everything for her and she wasn't thinking clearly yet, he reasoned.

"I'd like for you to stay here forever." Until he actually said it out loud, he hadn't realized the full extent of just how deep his feelings went. But there they were, out in the open. Completely exposed. There could be no confusion.

He waited for her reaction.

She smiled at the sentiment. So he wasn't throwing her out. "Thank you, but I can't stay at your house indefinitely."

"I'm not talking about my house, although—" he considered the statement for a moment "—that would be the logical progression now that you mention it."

Claire turned to him. She wasn't clearheaded tonight, but he had lost her. Completely. "Are we talking about the same thing?"

He decided to make it easy and spelled it out for her. "I'm talking about you going back to the order. What are you talking about?"

"I thought you meant my being here. Physically," she emphasized. For the first time since she'd gotten the call from Nancy, she allowed herself a small laugh.

"Not a bad topic," he allowed, a sensual smile on his lips. Because, ultimately, he was talking about her remaining—physically—in his life. In their lives, his and Danny's. Before he got sidetracked again, Caleb got down to the heart of the matter. "But I heard you, earlier, with your mother. I was in the hall, debating whether to come in or just wait outside until you came out. I heard your mother ask you to promise that you'd go back to being a nun—"

"A sister," she corrected.

"Whatever. It all boils down to you leaving Bedford again." *To you leaving me. Again.*

Well, that cleared things up, she thought. Claire shook her head. "I don't know what I'm going to do," she admitted. Everything was so up in the air. She needed to get through the funeral first, then tackle the rest of her life. "But to answer your question, no, I'm not going back to the order." In an odd way God had given her His answer. Her mother was gone. He didn't want her returning to the order. She was certain that it would be compounding a mistake to return.

Caleb narrowed his eyes, confused. "Then you lied to your mother?"

Not that he objected, since this was a lie he could more than live with, but he just hadn't thought that Claire was capable of actually lying to someone, especially her mother, on what amounted to her deathbed. He knew how much truth meant to her.

Claire didn't see it as lying. "I helped my mother die in peace. She kept blaming herself for my leaving the order and she actually felt that God was angry at her. She didn't listen all those times I tried to explain it to her and I didn't want her to die troubled."

Die.

Her mother was dead.

It was still so hard for her to comprehend. It felt so surreal. And she, heaven help her, felt so lost.

It had been a very long time since he'd felt a genuine smile blooming within him. He felt one now as he looked at Claire. "So you're not going back."

She slowly shook her head, underscoring her decision. "No, I'm not going back."

"Good." She looked at him in surprise. "Because I don't want you to."

She smiled to herself. Well, that was nice. It still didn't set her on a clear-cut path, but it was a nice thing to hear.

"So what would you suggest I do?" she asked, staring up at the dark sky. She ran her hands along her arms. She wore a sweater, but the evening chill had woven its way through it.

"Marry me."

Her head swung around at the same time that her jaw dropped. And then she collected herself, a small laugh surfacing along with renewed control.

"I think my hearing must be going. I thought I just heard you say 'Marry me.'"

"You did." He put his arms around her to warm her up. "Because I did."

Why had he said that? He'd never even told her that

he loved her. Was he trying to console her? "Is that your way of trying to help me deal with my grief?"

"Actually, it's a way to help me deal with mine. Ever since you came back to Bedford, you've managed to stir things up. Crack all the walls that were in place inside me. You've changed everything. You've put me back in touch with my son and made me wake up in the morning not regretting that I'm still alive, still breathing.

"You've made me feel things—made me *want* to feel things. That's why, when I heard you talking to your mother, promising her that you'd go back to the order, I wanted to run in and tell you that you couldn't do it, couldn't go."

"But you didn't," she pointed out, wondering what had stopped him.

"No, I didn't."

"Why?"

"Because if that was what you really wanted, if that was what you thought would make you happy, then I couldn't stand in your way." He looked at her for a long moment. Then said the words that instantly shot into her heart. "Because I love you. I always have."

It took her a second to catch her breath. When she did, she spoke in slow, measured cadence. "I made a deal with God this morning." She avoided looking at him. "I know it sounds silly, but it was something I used to do as a kid and I was desperate. I said to Him that if He cured my mother, I would take it as a sign that I was supposed to return to the order. But He didn't cure her," she said in a small voice. "He took her. So that either means that He hadn't heard me at all— or that He wants me to stay outside the order. When she died right in front of me, I wasn't sure just what the plan for the rest of my life was." She turned to him. "But now I am."

He was trying his best to follow her. "So you're saying that you think this was all prearranged, pre-destined or whatever the philosophy about having your fate cast in stone is called."

"What I'm saying," she replied with a wide smile, "is 'yes.'"

"Despite the so-called 'age difference'?" he wanted to know, taking her into his arms.

She shrugged. "Like you said, it isn't that much of a difference anymore. There's only one thing that makes a difference."

He kissed the top of her head before asking, "And that is?"

"That you love me."

"And?" he coaxed.

Her smile was warm and all encompassing. It was true, she thought. When one door closed, another opened. And this one was standing wide open, waiting for her to walk through. "And that I love you."

"Good answer," he told her just before he kissed her to seal the bargain.

And the rest of their lives together.

* * * * *

*Don't miss Marie Ferrarella's next romance,
CAVANAUGH PRIDE, available August 2009 from
Silhouette Romantic Suspense.*

*Celebrate 60 years of pure reading pleasure with
Harlequin!*

To commemorate the event, Harlequin Intrigue®
is thrilled to invite you to the wedding of The
Colby Agency's J. T. Baxley and his bride, Eve
Mattson.

That is, of course, if J.T. can find the woman who
left him at the altar. Considering he's a private
investigator for one of the top agencies in the
country—the best of the best—that shouldn't be
a problem. The real setback is that his bride isn't
who she appears to be…and her mysterious past
has put them both in danger.

*Enjoy an exclusive glimpse of Debra Webb's latest
addition to*
THE COLBY AGENCY: ELITE RECONNAIS-
SANCE DIVISION

THE BRIDE'S SECRETS

Available August 2009 from Harlequin Intrigue®.

The dark figures on the dock were still firing. The bullets cutting through the surface of the water without the warning boom of shots told Eve they were using silencers.

That was to her benefit. Silencers decreased the accuracy of every shot and lessened the range.

She grabbed for the rocks. Scrambled through the darkness. Bumped her knee on a boulder. Cursed.

Burrowing into the waist-deep grass, she kept low and crawled forward. Faster. Pushed harder. Needed as much distance as possible.

Shots pinged on the rocks.

J.T. scrambled alongside her.

He was breathing hard.

They had to stay close to the ground until they reached the next row of warehouses. Even though she was relatively certain they were out of range at this point, she wasn't taking any risks. And she wasn't slowing down.

J.T. had to keep up.

The splat of a bullet hitting the ground next to Eve had her rolling left. Maybe they weren't completely out of range.

She bumped J.T. He grunted.

His injured arm. Dammit. She could apologize later.

Half a dozen more yards.

Almost in the clear.

As she reached the cover of the alley between the first two warehouses she tensed.

Silence.

No pings or splats.

She glanced back at the dock. Deserted.

Time to run.

Her car was parked another block down.

Pushing to her feet, she sprinted forward. The wet bag dragged at her shoulder. She ignored it.

By the time she reached the lot where her car was parked, she had dug the keys from her pocket and hit the fob. Six seconds later she was behind the wheel. She hit the ignition as J.T. collapsed into the passenger seat. Tires squealed as she spun out of the slot.

"What the hell did you do to me?"

From the corner of her eye she watched him shake his head in an attempt to clear it.

He would be pissed when she told him about the tranquilizer.

She'd needed him cooperative until she formulated a plan. A drug-induced state of unconsciousness had been the fastest and most efficient method to ensure his continued solidarity.

"I can't really talk right now." Eve weaved into the right lane as the street widened to four lanes. What she needed was traffic. It was Saturday night—shouldn't be that difficult to find as soon as they were out of the old warehouse district.

A glance in the rearview mirror warned that their unwanted company had caught up.

Sensing her tension, J.T. turned to peer over his left shoulder.

"I hope you have a plan B."

She shot him a look. "There's always plan G." Then she pulled the Glock out of her waistband.

Cutting the steering wheel left, she slid between two vehicles. Another veer to the right and she'd put several cars between hers and the enemy.

She was betting they wouldn't pull out the fire-power in the open like this, but a girl could never be too sure when it came to an unknown enemy.

Deep blending was the way to go.

Two traffic lights ahead the marquis of a movie theater provided exactly the opportunity she was looking for.

The digital numbers on the dash indicated it was just past midnight. Perfect timing. The late movie would be purging its audience into the crowd of teenagers who liked hanging out in the parking lot.

She took a hard right onto the property that sported a twelve-screen theater, numerous fast-food hot spots and a chain superstore. Speeding across the lot, she selected a lane of parking slots. Pulling in as close to the theater entrance as possible, she shut off the engine and reached for her door.

"Let's go."

Thankfully he didn't argue.

Rounding the hood of her car, she shoved the Glock into her bag, then wrapped her arm around J.T.'s and merged into the crowd.

With her free hand she finger-combed her long hair. It was soaked, as were her clothes. The kids she bumped into noticed, gave her death-ray glares.

They just didn't know.

As she and J.T. moved in closer to the building, she grabbed a baseball cap from an innocent bystander. The crowd made it easy. The kid who owned the cap had made it even easier by stuffing the cap bill-first into his waistband at the small of his back.

Pushing through the loitering crowd, she made her way to the side of the building next to the main entrance. She pushed J.T. against the wall and dropped her bag to the ground. Peeled off her tee and let it fall.

His gaze instantly zeroed in on her breasts, where the cami she wore had glued to her skin like an extra layer. A zing of desire shot through her veins.

Not the time.

With a flick of her wrist she twisted her hair up and clamped the cap atop the blond mass.

"They're coming," J.T. muttered as he gazed at some point beyond her.

"Yeah, I know." She planted her palms against the wall on either side of him and leaned in. "Keep your eyes open. Let me know when they're inside."

Then she planted her lips on his.

* * * * *

Will J.T. and Eve be caught in the moment?
Or will Eve get the chance to reveal all of her
secrets?
Find out in
THE BRIDE'S SECRETS
by Debra Webb
Available August 2009 from Harlequin Intrigue®.

We'll be spotlighting a different series every month throughout 2009 to celebrate our 60th anniversary.

LOOK FOR
HARLEQUIN INTRIGUE®
IN AUGUST!

To commemorate the event, Harlequin Intrigue® is thrilled to invite you to the wedding of the Colby Agency's J.T. Baxley and his bride, Eve Mattson.

Look for *Colby Agency: Elite Reconnaissance*

THE BRIDE'S SECRETS
BY DEBRA WEBB

Available August 2009

www.eHarlequin.com

HIBPA09

Harlequin® Historical
Historical Romantic Adventure!

From *USA TODAY* bestselling author
Margaret Moore

THE VISCOUNT'S KISS

When Lord Bromwell meets a young woman on the mail coach to Bath, he has no idea she is Lady Eleanor Springford—until *after* they have shared a soul-searing kiss!

The nature-mad viscount isn't known for his spontaneous outbursts of romance—and the situation isn't helped by the fact that the woman he is falling for is fleeing a forced marriage....

The Viscount and the Runaway...

*Available August 2009
wherever you buy books.*

You're invited to join our Tell Harlequin Reader Panel!

By joining our new reader panel you will:

- Receive Harlequin® books—they are FREE and yours to keep with no obligation to purchase anything!
- Participate in fun online surveys
- Exchange opinions and ideas with women just like you
- Have a say in our new book ideas and help us publish the best in women's fiction

In addition, you will have a chance to win great prizes and receive special gifts! See Web site for details. Some conditions apply. Space is limited.

To join, visit us at
www.TellHarlequin.com.

REQUEST YOUR FREE BOOKS!
2 FREE NOVELS PLUS 2 FREE GIFTS!

SPECIAL EDITION®
Life, Love and Family!

YES! Please send me 2 FREE Silhouette Special Edition® novels and my 2 FREE gifts (gifts are worth about $10). After receiving them, if I don't wish to receive any more books, I can return the shipping statement marked "cancel." If I don't cancel, I will receive 6 brand-new novels every month and be billed just $4.24 per book in the U.S. or $4.99 per book in Canada. That's a savings of at least 15% off the cover price! It's quite a bargain! Shipping and handling is just 50¢ per book.* I understand that accepting the 2 free books and gifts places me under no obligation to buy anything. I can always return a shipment and cancel at any time. Even if I never buy another book from Silhouette, the two free books and gifts are mine to keep forever.

235 SDN EYN4 335 SDN EYPG

Name	(PLEASE PRINT)	
Address		Apt. #
City	State/Prov.	Zip/Postal Code

Signature (if under 18, a parent or guardian must sign)

Mail to the **Silhouette Reader Service**:
IN U.S.A.: P.O. Box 1867, Buffalo, NY 14240-1867
IN CANADA: P.O. Box 609, Fort Erie, Ontario L2A 5X3

Not valid to current subscribers of Silhouette Special Edition books.

Want to try two free books from another line?
Call 1-800-873-8635 or visit www.morefreebooks.com.

* Terms and prices subject to change without notice. Prices do not include applicable taxes. Sales tax applicable in N.Y. Canadian residents will be charged applicable provincial taxes and GST. Offer not valid in Quebec. This offer is limited to one order per household. All orders subject to approval. Credit or debit balances in a customer's account(s) may be offset by any other outstanding balance owed by or to the customer. Please allow 4 to 6 weeks for delivery. Offer available while quantities last.

Your Privacy: Silhouette is committed to protecting your privacy. Our Privacy Policy is available online at www.eHarlequin.com or upon request from the Reader Service. From time to time we make our lists of customers available to reputable third parties who may have a product or service of interest to you. If you would prefer we not share your name and address, please check here. ☐

SSE09R